"I'll pay you back when I've found a job."

Suzannah saw the professor's faint smile and blushed. "But you have no idea how awkward it is when one hasn't a penny piece in the world."

"My fault—I overlooked that fact when you came here," he said. "I do apologize."

"Oh, I'm not blaming you, indeed I'm not. You've done so much for me, and really it must be so vexing for you—my always turning up to annoy you."

He came and sat down opposite her. "But you don't annoy me, Suzannah. Indeed, I find that I miss you."

A great surge of love threatened to explode in her chest, but she kept her face calm. "Well, perhaps you do, like missing an aching tooth."

Betty Neels is well-known for her romances set in the Netherlands, which is hardly surprising. She married a Dutchman and spent the first twelve years of their marriage living in Holland and working as a nurse. Today she and her husband make their home in a small ancient stone cottage in England's West Country, but they return to Holland often. She loves to explore tiny villages and tour privately owned homes there, in order to lend an air of authenticity to the background of her books.

Books by Betty Neels

Don't miss any of our special offers. Write to us at the following address for information on our newest releases.

Harlequin Reader Service
901 Fuhrmann Blvd., P.O. Box 1397, Buffalo, NY 14240
Canadian address: P.O. Box 603,
Fort Erie, Ont. L2A 5X3

The Chain of Destiny

Betty Neels

Harlequin Books

TORONTO • NEW YORK • LONDON
AMSTERDAM • PARIS • SYDNEY • HAMBURG
STOCKHOLM • ATHENS • TOKYO • MILAN

Original hardcover edition published in 1989
by Mills & Boon Limited

ISBN 0-373-03053-3

Harlequin Romance first edition May 1990

CHAPTER ONE

THE rose bricks of the gracious old manor house shone warmly in the late August sunshine, and the small groups of people walking towards it paused to admire the pleasant sight; it wasn't one of the great country houses but it was early Tudor, still occupied by the descendants of the man who had built it and well worth a pleasant drive through the Wiltshire countryside on a bright afternoon.

There were still ten minutes before the door, solid wood in its stone archway, would be opened, and the visitors strolled around, studying the latticed windows and black and white plasterwork which presented a picture of enduring peace.

Appearances could be deceptive; behind its serene front there was a good deal of activity. The family had retired to their private wing, leaving a number of people to organise the afternoon. Mr Toms, the estate steward, was in charge; a small wiry man, familiar with the house down to its last creaking floorboard, he was counting small change into a box on the table just inside the door, ready for the vicar's wife, who would be issuing tickets. And disposed around the large square entrance hall stood the guides: Miss Smythe, the church school teacher, tall and thin with a ringing voice which allowed no tourist to dawdle or lose interest; Mrs Coffin, who ran the village stores and post office, and lastly Suzannah Lightfoot, whose aunt lived in the front lodge, offered to her for her lifetime after years of devoted duty to the family's great-aunt, who had lived to a great age and been something of a trial to them all. The family were seldom all there any more; the house was lived in by a peppery old uncle and his niece, a young woman of twenty-five or so, whose parents were living in America where her father had a diplomatic post. In the meantime the house was kept in good shape—helped by the modest number of visitors who came at weekends—ready for when the younger members of the family should return.

Mr Toms was frowning and tut-tutting. He had omitted to bring a spare roll of tickets with him, and there were barely five minutes before the door would be opened. He beckoned to Suzannah, gave her hurried directions and sent her off with an urgent wave of the hand.

She knew the old house well; two years ago she had been taken on as one of the house guides and, since she couldn't leave her aunt for any length of time, the small job suited her well enough. True, there was little money to be had from it, but what there was served to pay for her scant wardrobe and a few extras for her aunt, and she was a girl who made the best of what she had. Not that that was much.

She nipped up the worn treads of the oak staircase and along a wide corridor leading to the wing where the family lived and where Mr Toms had his office. It meant going through the picture gallery with its rows of paintings and dark oak wall tables and beautifully carved Jacobean chairs, isolated by crimson ropes, which she dusted twice a week. It was a gallery she loved, but she didn't waste time on it now, opening a little door in the panelled wall and hurrying along a small passage to Mr Toms' office. The roll of tickets was on his desk, so she picked it up closed the door behind her and started back again, a rather small girl with no pretentions to beauty, although her grey eyes were large and clear and her mouth, rather on the large side, curved up at its corners very sweetly. Her figure was pretty, but hardly showed to its best advantage in the checked cotton blouse and plain dark skirt; all the same, she was as neat as a new pin and her hair, richly red and shining, was tied back in a ponytail. She whisked through the door in the wall, closing it behind her, and then stopped short. Half-way down the gallery a man stood studying one of the portraits on the wall, and as she looked he began to stroll towards her. He was a large man, and tall, and certainly not in his first youth, for his hair was silvered at the temples and he had an air of assurance; he was also well-dressed in a casual way.

Probably sneaked in ahead of the rest, decided Suzannah, advancing towards him. She said politely, 'I'm sure you aren't aware that this part of the house is private? If you will come with me, I'll show you where the entrance is and you can join up with a guided party.'

He had come to a halt before her, studying her down his high-bridged nose with eyes as cold as blue ice. She bore this scrutiny with equanimity, although she went rather pink under it, especially when he asked indifferently, 'And what makes you think that I wish to be guided?'

She answered with tart politeness, 'It says very clearly at the door that visitors must take a guided tour, so perhaps you would come with me?'

'Are you a guide?'

'Yes.' She led the way through the gallery, paused at the end of the corridor to make sure that he was still behind her, and went down the staircase, where she left him with a firm, 'You may join any of the guided groups—you'll need a ticket.'

She turned away, but he put out a large, well-kept hand and took her gently by the elbow. 'Tell me,' he said softly, 'are you the local schoolteacher, or, if not that, the vicar's daughter?'

Suzannah lifted his hand off her arm and said with dignity, 'You are a very rude man.' She added with a tolerant matter-of-factness, 'Such a pity.'

The first of the visitors were being admitted; she handed over the tickets to the vicar's wife and went to stand in her appointed place to the left of the massive carved table in the centre of the hall. One by one she was joined by sightseers; each guide took from six to twelve visitors at a time, and today, with the summer holidays nearly over, there were fewer tourists; another month and the house would be closed for the winter. Suzannah, waiting patiently for the last of her group, allowed herself to worry about getting a job to take her through the months until the house opened again at Easter.

The guides were setting off, each on her own itinerary, and Suzannah counted heads, wished everyone a good afternoon and led the way out of the hall into the panelled dining-room, closely followed by an elderly couple, a stout man in a cloth cap, a thin lady in a hard felt hat, a pair of teenagers carrying a transistor radio and, last but by no means least, a tired-looking young woman carrying a fretful baby. Suzannah smelled trouble ahead, either from the baby or the transistor radio, but they had paid their money and they expected value for it. She exchanged a sympathetic smile with the young woman and took her stand by the table in the centre of the room. She laid a loving hand on its age-old patina. 'Elizabethan,' she began in her lovely clear voice, 'the carving is beautiful, and you will notice the bulbous legs, reflecting the clothes of that period; the oak cupboard is a court cupboard of the same period . . .' Her listeners crowded around as she pointed out the great silver salt-cellar, the engraved silver tankards and the silver sweetmeat boxes arranged on it. By the time they had reached the two-tiered chimneypiece they were beginning to show a faint interest and, much encouraged, she urged them to view the ceiling. 'Strapwork,' she recited, 'with a central motif of the ship of the Jacobean period. The same ship is carved above the door we are about to go through.'

Heads were lowered obediently as she led the way to the door, opened it and stood beside it to make sure that everyone went through. The last one was the man from the picture gallery, who despite his great size had managed to join the tail end of the group without her seeing him.

She gave him a chilly look as he went past her.

The dining-room led into the drawing-room, rather more William and Mary than Elizabethan, and here there was a good deal more to see. Suzannah went from the side-table with barley-sugar legs—these called forth a joke from the man in the cloth cap—to a Charles the Second armchair in walnut and cane, and a Gibbons chimneypiece. She loved the room and would have lingered in it, but her group were only vaguely interested, although they obediently followed her from one portrait to the next, commenting upon the opulent charms of the ladies in them and making outspoken remarks about the gentlemen's wigs, and all the while the man from the gallery wandered around on his own, but never so far that she felt that she must beg him to keep up with everyone else. A tiresome person, she reflected, leading her party across a handsome inner hall and into the ballroom.

It was here that the three guides met and passed each other and here, naturally enough, that the laggards wandered off with the wrong lot. Today there was the added complication of the baby beginning to cry. Its thin whimper gradually gathered strength until it was a piercing scream. Suzannah, gathering her little party together to move out of the ballroom and into the library, waited until the woman passed her.

'Look, why don't you sit down for a minute while I talk? We always allow a few extra minutes in the library, there's a lot to see.'

The woman looked very tired and pale. 'You don't mind?' she whispered and, rather to Suzannah's astonishment, handed her the baby.

It stopped crying at once, stared up at her with large blue eyes and sank into instant sleep. No one seemed to have noticed; she tucked the infant firmly against her shoulder and made her way from one visitor to the next, answering questions and pointing out the massive bookcases, the library steps and the enormous painting on one wall depicting the ancestor of the present owner, sitting on his charger, and staring in a noble fashion into the middle distance.

An eye on her watch told her that she was a little behind schedule; she nipped smartly to where the woman was sitting and handed back the baby and turned away to collect up the others. The man from the gallery was leaning nonchalantly against one wall, his hands in his pockets, watching her and smiling. It wasn't a nice smile, she thought, and to her annoyance she blushed.

There was only the inner staircase, the state bedroom and the boudoir to visit now. They straggled up the staircase, not really listening to her careful description of its wrought-iron balustrade, nor were they interested in the coffered ceiling, but the bedroom they enjoyed, admiring the great four-poster with its brocade hangings, and the silver jug and ewer on the little oak table with the silver mirror hanging above it. And the boudoir was admired as much and at even greater length, for it was furnished at a later period, with hanging cabinets, a chaise-longue, and some pretty shield-back armchairs. But at length she was able to collect everyone and lead them back down the main staircase to the hall, trying to ignore the man who, most annoyingly, wandered along at his own pace and, when they reached the hall, disappeared completely.

'And good riddance,' muttered Suzannah, wishing everyone goodbye.

The next group was already forming, a quite different kettle of fish, she saw at once: a donnish-looking elderly gentleman accompanied by a staid wife, and two stout ladies carrying books on antiques. It was nice to have an attentive audience, and she enjoyed herself, although just once or twice she found herself wishing that the strange man had been there too. But there was no sign of him. She escorted two more groups round the house before the door was finally shut and, after doing a round to make sure that everything was as it should be, and checking the takings with the vicar's wife, she walked down the drive, took a short-cut through the dense shrubbery half-way down its length, and reached the small grass clearing enclosed by a plain iron fence. She stood alongside the gate, a handsome edifice of wrought iron between two stone pillars, lichen-encrusted and topped by griffons. The lodge was a picturesque cottage, built for outward effect, and quite charming with its small latticed windows, miniature gabled roof and tall, twisted chimneys. Inside, the rooms were poky and dark, and the plumbing was in need of modernisation. All the same, it had been home to Suzannah for several years now, ever since her parents had died in a motoring accident while she was at boarding-school. Aunt Mabel had just retired and had offered her a home at once, and Suzannah had left the school and her hopes of a university and gone to live with her. Any vague ideas she had had about her future were squashed within a few months when her aunt became ill and it was found that she had a cerebral tumour. Inoperable, they had said, and sent her home again under the care of her doctor and with instructions to Suzannah not to tell her aunt what ailed her.

There was a small pension, plus Suzannah's small earnings to live on, and the cottage was rent-free; they managed very well, and the tumour, slow-growing, seemed quiescent except for the headaches it caused.

Suzannah, now twenty-two, had accepted her life sensibly, thankful that her aunt was still able to potter around and take pleasure from their quiet way of living, and if sometimes she regretted the future she had planned for herself, she never gave a sign that it was so. Only now, as she opened the door, she was wondering how she could best find a job which would allow her to be with her aunt for most of the day. But nothing of her worries showed as she went inside. The door opened directly on to the sitting-room, simply furnished but comfortable with a door leading to the small kitchen beyond. Another door in the wall opened on to the narrow stairs which led to the two bedrooms above; a narrow shower-room and toilet had been built on behind the kitchen when her aunt had gone there to live, and beyond that there was the garden where between them they grew vegetables and flowers, which Suzannah heaped into buckets and boxes and left at the gate in the hope that the visitors might buy them. Which they very often did, but now the summer was beginning to fade there was little to sell.

Her aunt was sitting in her chair with her cat, Horace, on her lap. She turned her head and smiled at Suzannah as she went in; she had a nice smile, which made her lined face looked years younger.

'There you are, dear. Did you have a busy afternoon?'

'Just busy enough to make it interesting,' said Suzannah cheerfully. Her eye fell on the table. 'You haven't had tea?'

Her aunt looked apologetic. 'Well, dear, I did get up to make a cup, but I had to sit down again. It's so silly, but I'm a little dizzy . . .'

Suzannah whisked across to her chair. 'Only dizzy?' she asked gently. 'No headache?'

'No, dear, just a dull, heavy feeling. I'd love a cup of tea.'

They had their tea and presently her aunt dozed off, which left Suzannah free to get their supper, feed Horace and shut up the few hens at the end of the garden. Supper was cooked and the table laid before her aunt awoke and sat down at the table. But she ate very little and presently said that she would go to bed.

'You're still dizzy?' asked Suzannah. 'I'll come up with you, Aunty, and if you're not better in the morning I'll get Dr Warren to call. Perhaps your tablets are too strong.'

She stayed upstairs until her aunt had fallen asleep and then cleared away their supper, laid the table for breakfast, settled Horace for the night and took herself off to bed, worried about her aunt. True, she had been known to have dizzy spells before, but they were over quickly, and this evening her aunt had looked ill and pale.

She crossed the tiny landing and made sure that her aunt was asleep before she got into bed herself. It took her a long time to go to sleep, and when she did she dreamed of her aunt and, inexplicably, of the man in the picture gallery.

It was a crisp, bright morning when she got up. She hung out of her small window to admire the trees beyond the meadow at the back of the cottage. She put on her dressing-gown and crossed the landing, to find her aunt wide awake.

She was still very pale, Suzannah saw uneasily, but all the same she said cheerfully, 'Did you have a good night, Aunty? I'll get you a cup of tea . . .'

Her aunt peered at her. 'Not tea, dear, I don't feel quite the thing—it's so silly to feel giddy when I'm lying in bed, isn't it?'

She began to sit up in bed and then with a muttered, 'Oh, dear', slid back against her pillows. 'Such a bad headache,' she whispered, 'and I feel so sick.'

Suzannah fetched a bowl, made her aunt comfortable and murmured in a reassuring way and when, surprisingly, her aunt went suddenly to sleep, she leapt down the stairs to the phone, a modern blessing which had been installed when her aunt had first become ill. It was barely seven o'clock, but she had no hesitation in ringing Dr Warren; he had told her to do just that if he was needed, and she wasn't a girl to panic and call him for something trivial.

His quiet voice assured her that he would be with her in ten minutes before he hung up.

He was as good as his word, and by then her aunt was deeply asleep. 'More than sleep,' he told her, 'a coma, not very deep as yet.' He looked at the small figure standing before him. 'Your aunt is too ill to move. Do you think you can manage?'

'Yes, of course—if you'll tell me what I have to do?'

'Very little.' He explained what needed to be done. 'And I'll get the district nurse to pop in later on.' He hesitated. 'I've an old friend staying with me for a couple of days—he's a friend of the Davinishes at the manor, too—he's a brain surgeon—I'd like him to take a look at your aunt, there might be something . . .'

'Oh, please—if there's anything at all . . . You see, she's been quite well for months and it's been hard to remember that she's ill. She's been getting slower and more tired, but never like this.' She shivered and the doctor patted her shoulder.

'Get yourself dressed and have some breakfast, I'll be back in an hour or two and see what can be done.'

He was as good as his word; she barely had the time to dress, bathe her sleeping aunt's face and hands and straighten the bed, feed a disgruntled Horace and make herself some tea before he was back, this time with his friend and colleague. The man from the picture gallery, coming quietly into the cottage, greeting her gravely and giving no sign at all that he had already met her.

But in any case Suzannah was too worried to give much thought to that; she led the way upstairs and stood quietly by while he examined her aunt with unhurried care and then trod downstairs again where he conferred quietly with Dr Warren. When they had finished Dr Warren called Suzannah from the kitchen, where she had been making coffee.

'Professor Bowers-Bentinck thinks that the wisest course for us to follow is to let your aunt remain here. There is no point in taking her to hospital; she is gravely ill—you do understand that, don't you? There is nothing to be done, my dear, and let us be thankful that she has slipped into a coma and will remain so . . .'

Suzannah gave a gulp. 'Until she dies?'

'Yes, Suzannah. Believe me, if there was the faintest hope of saving her by surgery, the professor would operate. I'm sorry.'

'How long?'

'A day—a few hours. I shall ask the district nurse to come here as soon as she has done her round. You will need help.'

All this while the professor has stood quietly by the window, looking out on to the little strip of grass and the flower border which separated the lodge from the drive. Now he turned to face her.

'I am so sorry, Miss Lightfoot, I wish that I could help, but Dr Warren is quite right, there is nothing to be done.'

He sounded so kind that she felt tears prick her eyes. It was hard to equate this calm, impersonal man with the hard-eyed, tiresome creature who had been in the picture gallery. She said in a small voice which she strove to keep steady, 'Thank you, I quite understand. It was good of you to come.' After a moment she added, 'Aunty will sleep? She won't wake and feel frightened?'

'She won't wake again,' he told her gently.

She nodded her untidy red head. 'I'll fetch the coffee.'

They drank it, sitting in the small room, the two men talking about nothing in particular, covering her silence, and presently the professor got to his feet and went back upstairs. When he came down again, the two men went away, getting into Dr Warren's elderly car with a final warning that she was to telephone and that Nurse Bennett would be with her directly.

Nurse Bennett had been the district nurse for years; the very sight of her comfortable form getting out of her little car was reassuring. She had known Miss Lightfoot for a long time and Suzannah for almost as long. She put her bag down on the sitting-room table and said cheerfully, 'Well, love, we've known this would happen—it doesn't make it any easier for you, but it's a gentle passing for your aunty, and we'd all wish for that, wouldn't we, after all she's done for others.'

Suzannah had a good cry on to her companion's plump shoulder and felt better for it. 'I'll make a pot of tea while you go upstairs,' she said in a watery voice, and managed a smile.

Miss Lightfoot slipped away as she slept, and by then it was late in the evening and Dr Warren had been once more. He had liked his patient and felt sorry for her niece. 'Nurse Bennett will stay here tonight,' he told Suzannah, 'and I'll deal with everything.'

He went back home and his wife asked him what would happen to Suzannah. 'She's a sensible girl', he observed. 'That's a nice little house and I dare say she'll find work; she's a clever girl, you know, should have gone to a university by rights. I dare say they'll give her a helping hand at the manor house.'

The professor had already left to keep an appointment; Dr Warren picked up the phone and left a message for him.

Almost the entire village went to the funeral. Miss Lightfoot had been liked by everyone, and Suzannah, going home to an empty little house, felt comforted by their kindness. She had refused several offers of hospitality; it would only be putting off the moment when she would be alone with Horace. She had been unhappy before when her parents had died, and she knew that the unhappiness would pass, and pass more quickly if she faced up to it and carried on with her life as usual. She cooked her supper, fed Horace, saw to the hens and went to bed, and if she cried a little before she slept, she told herself it was only because she was tired after a long and trying day.

It was hard at first and time hung heavy on her hands, for she had been doing more and more for her aunt during the past few months. She turned out cupboards and drawers, gardened for hours at a stretch, and in the evenings sat at the table, pondering ways and means. Her aunt had left only a very little money, for she had been supplementing her pension from her small capital. Suzannah had a few pounds saved, but she would have to find work as soon as possible. There had been a rumour in the village that Miss Smythe had asked for an assistant to help her in the school; Suzannah had had a good education, a clutch of A-levels and could have had a place in a university. Much cheered with the idea, she went to bed a week or so after her aunt's death, determined to go and see Miss Smythe in the morning.

She was up early to find that the postman had already been—several letters which she skimmed through and laid on one side to answer later; the last one was from the manor house and rather surprised her—a formal note asking her to call there that morning.

She read it a second time; perhaps there was a job for her there? She got dressed and had breakfast, tidied the little house and walked up the drive and round the side of the house to the door which the staff used. She met Mr Toms as she was going through the flagstoned passage which would lead her to the stairs and the private wing. She had always got on well with him, but now he showed no wish to stop and pass the time of day; indeed, he muttered that he was already late and barely paused to wish her good morning, which surprised her very much.

Grimm the butler answered the door when she pressed the discreetly hidden bell by the door at the top of the staircase. He bade her good morning, ushering her into a small ante-room, and then he went away, to return in a few minutes and ask her to go with him.

She had expected to see old Sir William, but there was no sign of him in the study into which she was ushered. Only his niece, a girl a little older than Suzannah, sat behind the desk. Suzannah had met her on several occasions and hadn't liked her; she liked her even less now as she went on writing, leaving Suzannah to stand in the middle of the room. She looked up finally and Suzannah thought what a pretty girl she was, tall and dark with regular features and blue eyes and always beautifully dressed. She said now, 'Oh, hello. Uncle isn't well enough to see anyone, so I've taken over for a time. I won't keep you long. I expect you've heard that there is an assistant teacher coming to live here to give Miss Smythe a hand. She'll start after half-term, in a couple of weeks' time, so we shall want the lodge for her to live in.'

It was the very last thing Suzannah had expected to hear. She was sensible enough to know that sooner or later she would have to leave the lodge unless she could get a job connected with the manor house, and somehow she had believed that old Sir William would have agreed to her applying for the post of teacher or at least allowed her to have stayed on and continued to work as a guide.

She said in a carefully controlled voice. 'I had hoped to apply for that post . . .'

'Well, it's been filled, and don't expect to find a job

here. Sir William has been far too easygoing; I'm cutting down on the staff. But you're able to shift for yourself, I suppose?' She gave Suzannah a cold smile. 'I consider that we've more than paid our debt to your aunt; there's no reason why we should have to go on paying it to you.' She pulled some papers towards her. 'Well, that's settled, isn't it? I don't know what you intend doing with your aunt's furniture—sell it to the schoolteacher if you like, only the lodge must be empty of your possessions in two weeks. Goodbye, Suzannah.'

Suzannah didn't answer, she walked out of the room and closed the door very gently behind her. It was like a bad dream, only it wasn't a dream, it was reality, and presently when she could think straight she would come to terms with it. Without thinking, she took the long way round to the front door, through the picture gallery, and half-way along it found herself face to face with Professor Bowers-Bentinck. She would have walked past him, but he put out a hand and stopped her, staring down at her pale, pinched face.

'Well, well, Miss Lightfoot, so we meet once more —there must be a magnet which draws us . . .' He had spoken lightly, but when she looked up at him with her lovely grey eyes full of hurt and puzzlement, he asked, 'What's wrong? You're not ill?'

She didn't answer, only pulled her arm away and ran from him, out of the gallery and down the stair-case, through the front door and down the drive. She would have to be alone for a while to pull herself together and then think what was best to do. Fleetingly she wondered why the professor was at the manor house, and then she remembered that old Sir William wasn't well. And anyway, what did it matter?

Back at the lodge, she sat down at the kitchen table with Horace on her lap and tried to think clearly. Two weeks wasn't long, but if she was sensible it would be time enough. She fetched pencil and paper and began to write down all the things which would have to be done.

The professor stood for a moment, watching Suzannah's flying figure, then he shrugged his huge shoulders and went back to the private wing, opened the door of the study and strolled in.

The girl at the desk looked up and smiled charmingly at him.

'Phoebe, I have just met that small red-haired girl who works as a guide here, with a face like skimmed milk and tragic eyes . . .'

The girl shrugged. 'Oh, she's that woman's niece—the one who died and lived at the lodge. The new assistant teacher will have to live there, so I've arranged for the girl to move out.'

He leaned against the wall, looking at her without expression. 'Oh? Has she somewhere to go?'

'How should I know, Guy? She's young and quite clever, so I've heard; she'll find something to do.'

'No family, no money?'

'How on earth should I know? Uncle William has been far too soft with these people.'

'So you have turned her loose into the world?'

The girl frowned. 'Well, why not? I want that lodge and there's no work for her as a guide—I've got rid of that woman from the post office, too. Miss Smythe can manage on her own, and if we get more visitors in the summer I'll get casual help.'

'Does your uncle know about this?' he spoke casually.

'Good heavens, no! He's too old to be bothered. I'll write to Father and let him know when I've got time.'

'And he will approve?'

She shrugged and laughed. 'It wouldn't matter if he didn't—he's on the other side of the world.' She pushed back her chair and smiled charmingly. 'Let's talk about something else, Guy—how about driving me over to Hungerford and giving me lunch?'

'Impossible, I'm afraid, Phoebe. I have to be back in town this afternoon.' He strolled back to the door. 'I came to see your uncle before I left.'

'You're not going? I counted on you staying for a few days . . .' She got up and crossed the room to him. 'You don't mean that?'

He had opened the door. 'My dear girl, you tend to forget that I work for a living.'

'You don't need to,' she retorted.

'Agreed, but it's my life.' He made no move to respond when she kissed his cheek.

'We'll see each other?' she asked.

'Undoubtedly, my dear.' He had gone, shutting the door behind him.

He went back to Dr Warren's house, made his farewells, threw his bag into the boot of the Bentley and drove away. But not very far. At the main gates of the manor house he stopped, got out and knocked on the lodge door. There was no answer, so he lifted the latch and walked in.

Suzannah was sitting at the table, neatly writing down what needed to be done if she were to leave in two weeks—the list was long and when she had finished it she began on another list of possible jobs she might be able to do. It seemed to her, looking at it, that all she was fit for was to be a governess—and were there such people nowadays? Or a mother's help, or find work in a hotel or large house as a domestic worker. Whichever way she looked at it, the list was depressing.

She looked up and saw him standing in the doorway, and for some reason she wanted to burst into tears at the sight of him. She said in a slightly thickened voice, 'Oh, do go away . . .'

Despite her best efforts, two large tears rolled down her cheeks.

'I'll go when I'm ready,' he told her coolly, 'and don't, for pity's sake, start weeping. It's a waste of time.'

She glared at him and wiped a hand across her cheeks like a child. She wasn't sure why he seemed to be part and parcel of the morning's miserable happening; she only knew that at that moment she didn't like him.

He pulled out a chair and sat down opposite her, stretching out his long legs before him. 'You have to leave here?'

'Yes.' She blew her nose and sat up very straight. 'Now, if you would go away, I have a great deal to do.'

He sat looking at her for a few moments, frowning a little, then shrugged his shoulders. 'Miss Davinish tells me that you have no job. Perhaps I could have helped in some way,' his blue eyes were cold, 'but it seems that I was mistaken.' He got to his feet. 'I'll bid you good day, young lady.'

He went away as quietly as he had come, and she heard his car drive away.

CHAPTER TWO

SUZANNAH did her best to shake off the feeling that the not very solid ground beneath her had been cut from under her feet. She might not like the professor, but he had offered to help her and she badly needed help, and like a fool she had turned his offer down; she hadn't even thanked him for it, either. A pity he hadn't had the patience to stay a little longer until her good sense had taken over from her stupid bout of weeping. She winced at the thought of the cold scorn in his eyes. And yet he had been so kind when Aunt Mabel had been ill . . .

As for the professor, he drove back to London, saw a handful of patients at his consulting rooms, performed a delicate and difficult brain operation at the hospital and returned to his elegant home in a backwater of Belgravia to eat his dinner and then go to his study to catch up on his post. But he made slow work of it. Suzannah's red hair, crowning her white, cross face, kept superimposing itself upon his letters. He cast them down at length and reached for the telephone as it began to ring. It was Phoebe at her most charming, and she had the knack of making him laugh. They talked at some length and he half promised to spend the next weekend at the manor house. As he put the phone down, he told himself that it was to be hoped that Suzannah would be gone.

He spoke so forcefully that Henry, his long-haired

dachshund, sitting under his desk, half asleep, came out to see what was the matter.

He had a long list the next day, and when it was over he sat in sister's office, drinking coffee and taking great bites out of the sandwiches she had sent for, listening courteously to her rather tart observations on lack of staff, not enough money and when was she to have the instruments she had ordered weeks ago?

'I'll see what I can do,' he told her. 'We need another staff nurse, don't we? We didn't get a replacement for Mrs Webb when she left. You're working at full stretch, aren't you, Sister?'

She gave him a grateful look. Sister Ash was in her fifties, a splendid theatre sister and, although she had a junior sister to take over when she was off duty, she was hard-pressed. Just like Professor Bowers-Bentinck to think of that, she reflected; such a nice man, always calm, almost placid when he was operating, and with such lovely manners. She thanked him and presently he went off to the intensive care unit to take a look at his patient. It was as he was strolling to the entrance, giving last minute instructions to his registrar, Ned Blake, that he stopped dead.

'Of course,' he murmured. 'Why didn't I think of it before?'

'A change in treatment?' asked Ned.

'No, no, my dear chap—nothing to do with our patient. Keep on as I suggest, will you? I'll be in the earliest I can in the morning, and give me a ring if you're worried.' He nodded goodbye and went out to his car and drove home, where he went straight to his study, sat in his chair for five minutes or more, deep in thought, and then picked up the phone.

The voice which answered him was elderly but brisk. 'Guy, dear boy, how nice to hear your voice; it would be nicer still to see you . . .'

He talked for a few minutes and the voice said cosily, 'Well, dear, what exactly do you want us to do?'

The Professor told her.

Suzannah spent several days packing up the contents of the cottage. There was little of value: a few pieces of jewellery which her aunt had possessed, one or two pieces of silver, a nice Coalport tea service . . . She put them into cardboard boxes and carried them down to the post office, where Mrs Coffin stowed them away safely in an attic. The new assistant teacher had called to see her too, and had been delighted to buy the furniture, which was old-fashioned but well-kept. Everything else Suzannah had promised to various people in the village. And, this done, she set to, writing replies to every likely job she could find advertised which could offer her a roof over her head. Several of her letters weren't answered, and those who did stated categorically that no pets were allowed. It was a blow, but she had no intention of abandoning Horace, so she wrote out an advertisement offering her services in any domestic capacity provided she might have a room of her own and Horace might be with her, and took it down to the post office.

Mrs Coffin, behind the counter, weighing out oatmeal for a beady-eyed old lady, greeted her with some excitement. 'Don't you go posting that letter, m'dear, not if it's a job—there's something in the local paper this morning . . .' She dealt with the old lady and then invited Suzannah to join her behind the counter. 'Just you look at that, love.' She folded the paper and pointed at the situations vacant column. 'Just up your street.'

Suzannah, with Mrs Coffin breathing gustily down her neck, obediently read. A competent, educated person was required for a period of two or three months to sort and index old family documents. An adequate salary would be paid and there was the use of a small flatlet. Pets not objected to. Good references were essential. Application in the first instance to be made in own handwriting. A box number followed.

'Well,' declared Suzannah and drew a great breath. 'Do you suppose it's real?'

'Course it is, m'dear. Now you just go into the room at the back and write a letter, and it'll go with the noon post.' Mrs Coffin rummaged through a shelf of stationery behind her. 'Here, take this paper, it's best quality and it will help to make a good impression.'

'References . . .'

'You can nip round to the vicar and Dr Warren when you've written it. You just sit yourself down and write.'

The dear soul pushed Suzannah into the little room at the back of the shop and pulled out a chair, and, since she had nothing to lose, she wrote.

Three days went by and, though she had made up her mind not to depend too much on a reply, she was disappointed to hear nothing. She got up early on the fourth morning and wrote out her own advertisement once more, and was putting it into an envelope when the postman pushed several letters through the letter-box. There were still outstanding matters arising from her aunt's death and, trivial though they were, she had dealt with them carefully; she leafed through the little bundle to discover most of them were receipts of the small debts she had paid, but the last letter was addressed in a spidery hand on thick notepaper and bore the Marlborough postmark.

Suzannah opened it slowly. The letter inside was brief and written in the same spidery hand, informing her that her application had been received and, since her references were satisfactory, would she be good enough to go to the above address for an interview in two days time? Her expenses would be paid. The letter was signed by Editha Manbrook, an elderly lady from the look of her handwriting, which, while elegant in style, was decidedly wavery.

Suzannah studied the address on the letter: Ramsbourne House, Ramsbourne St Michael. A village, if she remembered rightly, between Marlborough and Avebury. She could get a bus to Marlborough and probably a local bus to the village, which was only a few miles further on.

She went to Mrs Coffin's shop after breakfast, told her the good news and posted her reply, and then hurried back to the lodge to worry over her wardrobe. There wasn't all that much to worry about. It would have to be her tweed suit, no longer new, but with a good press it would pass muster; it was grey herringbone and did nothing to improve her looks, but on the other hand she considered that it made her look sober and serious, two attributes which would surely count when it came to selecting a candidate for the job? There was a grey beret to go with the suit, and a pair of well-brushed black shoes and her good leather handbag and gloves. She tried them all on to make sure that they looked all right, with Horace for an audience.

The appointment was for two o'clock; she had an early lunch, told Horace to be good while she was away, and caught the bus to Marlborough. There was a local bus going to Avebury several times a day and she caught it without trouble, arriving at Ramsbourne St Michael with time enough to enquire where Ramsbourne House was and then walk for ten minutes or so to the big gates at the end of a country lane.

The drive was a short one, running in a semicircle between shrubs, and it opened out before a pleasant Regency house, painted white and with wide sash-windows. The drive disappeared round one side, but Suzannah went to the canopied porch and rang the bell.

An elderly maid opened the door and Suzannah said, 'Perhaps I shouldn't have come to this door—I've come for an appointment about a job . . .'

The woman smiled and ushered her inside. 'That's right, miss, I'll show you where you can wait.'

She opened a door to one side of the entrance hall and Suzannah went past her into a pleasant room with wide windows overlooking the side of the house. She paused only for a moment, and then sat down in the nearest chair.

She hoped that her surprise hadn't shown too clearly upon her face; it had been foolish of her to suppose that she would be the only person after the job. She murmured a rather belated good afternoon and took a surreptitious stock of the other occupants of the room. There were four of them, and each of them had the look of a woman who was skilled at her work and knew it. One of them said loudly now, 'There is no mention of shorthand and typing, but I imagine it will be an absolute must for this kind of job.' The others agreed and Suzannah's heart sank into her shoes. Her journey was a waste of time; she could have put her advertisement in the paper three days ago and perhaps by now she would have had some replies; time was running out . . . She checked her thoughts; fussing wasn't going to help. She watched the other young women go in one after another until she sat alone, and presently the last one came out and gave her a cursory nod. 'You can go in.'

So Suzannah knocked on the door at the end of the room and went in. The room was large, opulently furnished in an old-fashioned style and very warm. Two old ladies sat on either side of a bright fire and neither spoke as she crossed the room over the polished wood floor towards them. When she was near enough she wished them a good afternoon in her quiet voice and stood patiently while they took a good look at her.

One of the old ladies took up her letter and read it. 'Suzannah Lightfoot? A pretty name. What do you know about cataloguing and indexing documents?'

'Nothing—that is, I have never done it before, but I think it must be largely a matter of common sense and patience. I'm interested in old books and papers, and I know I would very much like the work, but I can't do shorthand nor can I type.'

The second old lady said thoughtfully. 'From your references I see that you had a place offered you at Bristol University reading English Literature. You didn't mention that in your reply to my advertisement.' And when Suzannah didn't answer, 'Modesty is always refreshing. We think that you will be very suitable for the post. The salary we offer is by no means large; indeed, we were left with the impression that it is quite inadequate when it was mentioned to our other applicants. But there is a small flatlet where you may live while you are here.'

'I have a well-behaved cat,' said Suzannah.

'We have no objection to your pet, but perhaps you may object to the salary we offer.' She mentioned a sum which, while modest, was a good deal more than Suzannah had hoped for.

She said quickly, 'I'm quite satisfied with that, thank you, Miss Manbrook.'

'Then we shall expect you—let me see—in four days' time? I think it best if we send the car for you, since you will have luggage and your cat. We have your address, have we not?' She glanced at the other lady. 'You agree, Amelia?' and when that lady nodded, 'Then you will be good enough to press the bell; you will wish to see the flat.'

The same elderly maid answered it and led Suzannah away, back across the hall down a passage and out of a side door. The small courtyard outside was encircled with outbuildings: a garage with a flat above it, store-rooms and what could have been a stable, now empty. At the end of these there was a small door which her companion opened. There was a tiny hall leading to a quite large room with a cooking alcove in one corner and an open door leading to a small bathroom. There were windows back and front and a small Victorian fire-place. It was nicely furnished and carpeted and, although the front window looked out upon the court-yard and the side of the house, the view from the back window was delightful.

'Oh, how very nice,' said Suzannah, and beamed at her companion. 'Would you tell me your name?'

'Parsons, miss. And you've no call to be nervous; there's the cook's flat over the garage and the rest of us have got rooms on this side of the house.'

Her rather severe face broke into a smile. 'I was hoping it would be you, miss—didn't take a fancy to any of the other young women.'

'Why, thank you, Parsons. I'm quite sure I'm going to be very happy here. When I come in four days' time will you tell me where to go for meals and at what time?'

'It'll be Mr Snow to tell you that, miss—the butler, it's his day off but he'll be here when you come.'

'You've been very kind. Now I must go back and pack my things. Miss Manbrook . . .'

'Lady Manbrook, Miss.'

'Oh, I didn't know. She didn't mention when I would be fetched.'

'Mr Snow will let you know.'

'Oh, good.' At the door, on the point of leaving, she asked, 'And the other lady?'

'That's Lady Manbrook's sister, miss, Mrs van Beuck; they're both widowed.'

'Thank you, Parsons.' Suzannah glanced at her watch. 'I must catch my bus.' They wished each other goodbye and she went off down the drive and along the lane and found that she would have to wait ten minutes or so for a bus, which gave her the chance to think over her afternoon and dwell on the delights of the little flat.

Her friends in the village were glad when she told them her news. Mrs Coffin gave her an old cat basket for Horace, Dr Warren and his wife gave her a pretty eiderdown, and Miss Smythe presented her with a red geranium in a pot. Suzannah bade them all goodbye, cleaned the lodge ready for its new occupant, packed the last of her possessions and, obedient to Mr Snow's letter, stood ready and waiting by ten o'clock in the morning, Horace restless but resigned beside her in his basket.

It was a pity there was no one to see her leave, thought Suzannah, for the car which arrived was an elderly, beautifully maintained Daimler. The driver was a short, thick-set man, with grey hair, very smart in his dark grey uniform.

He replied in a friendly way to her good morning and added, 'Croft's the name, miss. I'll just put everything in the boot.' He eyed Horace, peering at him through the little window of his basket. 'You've got a cat there? He can go on the back seat.'

His wife was housekeeper for Lady Manbrook, he informed Suzannah as they drove; they had been there for twenty-five years and most of the staff had been there almost as long. 'I hope you like a quiet life, miss,' he observed, 'for there's nothing to do of an evening. Got a telly, have you?'

'No, I haven't, but I have got a little radio and I like reading. I'll be quite happy; I've lived in the country for some time and I like it.'

'Of course, there's guests from time to time, but mostly it's just the two ladies.'

She had been a little nervous of meeting Mr Snow, but she need not have been. True, he was very dignified and smiled seldom, but she felt that he approved of her. She was handed the key of her new home, her luggage and Horace were deposited in it and she was requested to present herself in half an hour in the front hall, when she would be taken to

Lady Manbrook.

Half an hour wasn't long in which to get settled in; Horace, set free and allowed to roam round the room, ate the snack she got for him and settled down on the window-sill beside the geranium, and she made herself a cup of coffee, tidied her already neat person and went across to the house.

The two old ladies didn't look as though they had moved since she had last seen them, only they wore different dresses. The butler ushered her in and Lady Manbrook said, 'Come and sit down, Miss Lightfoot. Snow, please bring coffee; we will lunch half an hour later than usual, that will give Miss Lightfoot time to unpack her things.'

Snow trod quietly away and Suzannah waited to see what was to happen next.

'When we have had coffee Snow will show you to the room where you will work,' said Lady Manbrook. 'The papers and diaries are in one of the attics; he will accompany you there and you may decide which of them you wish to begin work upon.'

'Some of them are most interesting, so I am told,' remarked Mrs van Beuck.

'Do you want to see any of them before I start?' asked Suzannah. 'There is nothing private . . . ?'

'I think not; if there is, I feel sure that you will inform me. All I require is that they should be put in some kind of order, and when that is done, I should like you to read them carefully and index them.'

'Are there many papers?'

'I have been told that there are two or three trunks. These things do tend to accumulate,' added Lady Manbrook vaguely. 'Ah, here is coffee. Be good enough to pour, Miss Lightfoot. We lunch at half-past one; you will, of course, join us.'

Suzannah thanked her nicely, drank her coffee and excused herself. If she looked sharp about it, she could unpack and get settled in, feed Horace properly and introduce him to his surroundings before then. And in the afternoon she would make a start on the contents of the attic. She found Snow waiting for her in the hall and they climbed the staircase at the back of the hall to the floor above, opened a door in a wall and climbed to the next floor and then once more mounted a very narrow, twisting staircase to the attics. Snow opened a door with a flourish and she went in. There were several attics, running the length of the house, connected by open archways, all well lit by dormer windows. The trunks were in the second, large and old-fashioned, made of leather and strapped tightly. They undid one of them between them and Suzannah got down on her knees to inspect the contents. There was no sort of order: bundles of letters, foolscap sheets tied with string, a number of what appeared to be diaries all jostled themselves together. It would be hard to know where to begin, she decided.

'Lady Manbrook said that you would show me where I could work, Mr Snow, but I think I shall have to do the sorting here. There's plenty of room and the light's good. When I've got things in a bit of order I can carry them to wherever I've to work and start the indexing.'

'Just as you say, miss. I will arrange for a small table and chair to be brought here, and anything else that you may require. I must say there appears to be a good deal of work involved.'

'Yes, I think so, too,' said Suzannah cheerfully, 'but I'm sure it will be interesting.' They went back down the little stairs and he showed her a room, very light and airy with a wide table and comfortable chair and an open hearth, in which, he pointed out, a fire would be lit while she was working there.

Her own little room seemed very small when she reached it, but decidedly cosy; it already looked like home, too, with the geranium on the window-sill and Horace curled up on one of the chairs. She unpacked her few things, fed him and took him outside for a short time and then tidied herself and went back to the house for lunch—a meal eaten in some state in a large, heavily furnished dining-room with a great deal of white damask and silver. After an initial shyness Suzannah began to enjoy herself; the two old ladies were charming, keeping up a gentle flow of conversation calculated to put her at her ease. She left them after they had had their coffee, took a quick look to see if Horace was comfortable, and then repaired to the attics.

It seemed at first glance a formidable task, but not a dull one. She opened the first trunk . . .

She was completely absorbed when Snow tapped on the door and brought her a tea-tray. She sat back on her heels and said apologetically, 'Oh, Mr Snow, I could have come down—I didn't know.' She smiled at him. 'I got rather carried away.'

He surveyed the neat rows of piled-up papers, old dance programmes, newspaper cuttings and the like. 'Indeed, miss, I can well understand that. It is no trouble to bring you a tea-tray. Dinner is at eight o'clock; the ladies go to dress just after seven o'clock.'

'Oh, but surely I'm not to dine with them?'

'Indeed you are, miss. They quite understand that you would not wish to join them for tea and interrupt your work, and breakfast is taken by the ladies in their beds. Your breakfast will be served in the morning-room at eight o'clock.'

'Thank you, Mr Snow.'

'And if you will not find it presumptuous, miss, you should address me as Snow.'

'Oh, but the maid who showed me to my room called you Mr Snow.'

'And quite rightly; I am in charge of the staff here and head of the domestics, but you, miss, are employed by Lady Manbrook.'

She said in her sensible way, 'Oh, I see, thank you for telling me. I'll try not to give any of you any extra work.'

'If I may say so, miss, it is a pleasure to have some one young in the house.'

He made his stately way out of the room, leaving her to enjoy tiny sandwiches, hot buttered toast and fairy cakes as light as air.

By seven o'clock she had the trunk empty, its contents extending in piles half-way across the attic floor. Tomorrow she would go through each pile and arrange the contents according to the dates, dealing with the newspaper cuttings first, for it seemed to her that they would be the easiest. There were two more trunks; she would have to sort them in the same way and then add the piles together. Weeks of work, if she was to index them too.

She went downstairs and through the side door to her flat, fed Horace and took him for a brief stroll, then came back to switch on the lights and draw the curtains.

A fire had been laid ready to light in the small grate and she put a match to it, put the fireguard in front of it and went to take a bath and dress. She had nothing really suitable for dinner, only a dark brown dress in fine wool, very plain and at least two years old, or a grey pinafore dress with a white silk blouse. She got into the brown, promising herself that with her first pay packet she would buy something suitable for dining in the splendour of Lady Manbrook's dining-room. She took pains with her face, brushed her tawny head until it shone like copper, and went back to the house to be met by Snow.

'The ladies expect you to join them in the drawing-room,' he offered, and led the way.

Suzannah saw at a glance that her brown dress was woefully inadequate, but she didn't allow it to worry her; she sat down to enjoy her sherry and take her sensible part in the conversation. And dinner, although somewhat more lengthy than lunch, was just as pleasant. She excused herself shortly afterwards, wished the two ladies goodnight and went back to her room. The fire was burning nicely and Horace was sitting before it, the picture of a contented cat. Suzannah too uttered a sigh of contentment, made a cup of tea from the selection of beverages she had found in the tiny cupboard in the kitchen corner, and went to bed. The room was warm and the firelight comforting, and she curled up and went to sleep within minutes, with Horace beside her.

Within a few days she had found her feet. She had little time to herself but that didn't matter overmuch; no one had suggested the hours she should work, so she arranged her own; from nine o'clock in the morning until lunchtime, and then work again without a pause until the seven o'clock gong. Horace, that most amenable of cats, was quite happy to have a walk in the morning after breakfast, another few minutes after lunch and then a more leisurely stroll in the evening. Snow had offered scraps from the kitchen: tasty morsels of chicken, ends off the joints and fish; and she had arranged to have milk left at her door from the local farm. Life might be busy, but it was pleasant, and she had no idle moments in which to repine. When the opportunity occurred, she would have to ask about having a half-day a week so that she could shop in Marlborough for her bits and pieces.

She thought that probably she was going about her task in a very unprofessional way but, be that as it may, she had made headway. The piles of letters, cuttings and old photographs were beginning to take shape and make sense.

Some of them were very old indeed; letters written in spidery hands, crossed and recrossed, invoices and bills, dressmaker's accounts and any number of receipts and recipes. She began to deal with these, getting them roughly into date order, separating them into heaps. It was slow work but she was methodical and very patient. She was able to tell Lady Manbrook that the last of the trunks had been emptied by the end of her first week; it had seemed a good opportunity to ask about her working hours, but before she could touch on the subject Mrs van Beuck observed, 'You will accompany us to church, my dear? The rector preaches an excellent sermon. You will come in the car with us, of course; it will be at the front door at half-past ten precisely.'

She looked across at her sister, who smiled and

nodded. 'We have discussed the matter,' she said, 'and we would prefer to call you by your Christian name if you have no objection?'

'Oh, I'd like you to. No one calls me Miss Lightfoot —well, almost no one.' She had a brief memory of Professor Bowers-Bentinck's cold voice uttering her name with what seemed to her to be mocking deliberation. And after that it hardly seemed the moment to bring up the matter of her free time. It was, after all, only a week since she had started work, and she was happy in her little flat and everyone was kind to her; even Snow, who could look so austere, had unbent sufficiently to save the best morsels for Horace. There was, of course, the little matter of when she would be paid. She had a little money, but it wouldn't last for ever. Perhaps Lady Manbrook intended to pay her when she had finished her work, but that would be a month or six weeks away, or even longer. There was no use worrying about it; she went back to the attic with the careful notes she had made to show Lady Manbrook and then made her way back to the flat to get ready for dinner.

She would have enjoyed the walk to church in the morning but, since she had been expected to accompany the ladies, she got into the old-fashioned car with them and was borne in some state to the village church. The family pew was at the front and the church was comfortably full; she was conscious of curious glances as she followed the two ladies down the aisle. After the service, as they made their stately progress to the church porch, she was introduced to the rector and a number of elderly people who made vague, kind enquiries about her without really wanting to know, so that she was able to murmur politely without telling them anything.

At lunch she made another effort to talk about her free time; indeed, she got as far as, 'I was wondering about my hours of work . . .' only to be interrupted by Lady Manbrook with a kindly,

'We have no intention of interfering, Suzannah. It is, I'm sure, most interesting and you enjoy it, do you not? And I must say that what you have told us about it, has whetted our appetites to know more about your finds. Perhaps you would take tea with us this afternoon and bring down those old dance programmes you were telling us about? We have tea at four o'clock, and it would be most amusing to go through them.'

'I haven't got them in order yet, Lady Manbrook . . .'

'You are so quick and efficient that I'm sure you can get them sorted out before tea.' The old lady smiled at her very kindly, so that Suzannah stifled a sigh and agreed.

So when she had fed Horace and taken him for his short trot, she went back to the attic once more. It was a lovely day, and a walk would have been very satisfying; she made up her mind to talk to Lady Manbrook when she went downstairs for tea.

She was on her knees, carefully sorting the old-fashioned dance programmes with their little pencils attached into tidy piles; most of them were late nine-teenth century and charming, and she lingered over some of them, trying to imagine the owners, picturing the quadrilles and polkas and waltzes they must have danced and their elaborate dresses. She was so absorbed that she didn't hear the door open, but a slight sound made her turn her head.

Professor Bowers-Bentinck was standing there,

leaning against the wall watching her.

'Well, well, this is a pleasant surprise.' His voice had a silkiness she didn't much like.

'A surprise,' she amended in her sensible way, 'but I don't know about it being pleasant.'

'An outspoken young lady,' he commented, 'but I should feel flattered that you remember me.'

She was still kneeling, a handful of programmes in her hand, looking at him. She said matter-of-factly, 'Well, I'd be silly if I didn't—you're much larger than most men, for a start, and you must know you're good-looking; besides that, you came to see Aunt Mabel.'

'Such an abundance of compliments,' he murmured.

'They're not meant to be,' said Suzannah prosaically, 'just facts.' She had a sudden alarming thought. 'Lady Manbrook—she's not ill? Or Mrs van Beuck? They were all right at lunch.' She sprang to her feet. 'Is that why you are here?'

'Both ladies are in splendid health', he assured her. He eyed her coldly. 'You are very untidy and dusty.'

'Of course I am, it's dusty work, and I have to get down on to the floor—there's more room, and anyway, I can't see that it matters to you.'

'It doesn't. Tell me, why do I find you here? How did you find this job?'

'It was advertised. I've been here a week, and I'm very happy.' She looked at him uncertainly. 'Do you mind telling me why you're here?'

'I've come to tea.'

Her lovely eyes grew round. 'Have you really? How extraordinary that we should meet again . . .'

'Yes, isn't it? You don't object?'

'Object? Why should I? I mean, one is always

bumping into people in unexpected places.'

'How true.' He eyed her frowningly. 'Had you not better finish and wash your hands and tidy your hair? It's almost four o'clock.'

She dusted her skirt and gave him a tolerant glance. 'Don't worry, I'll make myself presentable. I usually have my tea up here on a tray.' She added kindly, 'You don't need to fuss.'

His voice was as cold as his eyes. 'I'm not in the habit of fussing—what a tiresome girl you are.' He went through the door, closing it behind him, leaving her to gather up the programmes and then leave the attic after him. Undoubtedly a bad-tempered man, she reflected, and because of that to be pitied.

She told Horace all about him while she brushed her bright hair into smoothness, ready for tea.

CHAPTER THREE

THE drawing-room looked charming as she went in; the lamps were lit and the firelight flickered on the walls and twinkled on the silver muffin dish on the tea-table. The two ladies were sitting in their usual chairs, and lounging in an outsize armchair was the professor, looking very much at home.

An old friend, she wondered, or the family doctor? Quite obviously someone who knew the old ladies well.

He got to his feet as she crossed the room and drew forward a small armchair for her, and Lady Manbrook said, 'Our nephew tells us that he has met you previously, Suzannah, so there is no need to introduce you. I see that you have the dance programmes we were discussing with you; when we have had tea you must show them to us.'

Suzannah murmured a reply. Of course, now that she saw the three of them together there was no mistaking the relationship—those high-bridged, self-assured noses, the cool blue stare from heavy-lidded eyes. She sat composedly, drinking tea from paper-thin china and nibbling at minuscule cucumber sandwiches, and allowed her imagination to have full rein. The professor would live in London, because undoubtedly that was where a man of his ability would work, but he was friends—close friends, probably —with Phoebe Davinish. He would be spending the weekend with her, and had dropped in to say hello to his aunts.

She was brought up short by his voice, rather too smooth for her liking, wanting to know if she was enjoying her work.

'Very much, thank you,' she told him.

'And how long do you suppose it will take you to finish it?' he continued.

'I'm not sure. Everything is sorted into dated piles, but I think that is the easiest part; you see, the letters and cuttings are about a great many people—they'll have to be sorted out.'

'There is no hurry,' declared Mrs van Beuck. 'You seem to have accomplished a great deal in a week . . .'

'Even on a Sunday,' murmured the professor. 'Do you prefer to have a free day in the week?'

'Me?' Suzannah spoke sharply, with a fine disregard for grammar. 'I'm very happy——'

He cut her short. 'I'm sure you are; nevertheless, you should have time to yourself. I cannot imagine that my aunts will mind if you take a week or so longer with your sorting and indexing; I am equally sure that they would wish you to enjoy a certain amount of time to yourself.'

Lady Manbrook was looking quite upset. 'My dear child, how thoughtless of us—of course you must have some hours to yourself. What do you suggest, Guy?'

He didn't even look at Suzannah to see what she thought about it, which annoyed her. 'Oh, a day off each week—most office workers and shop assistants have two days—and set hours of work each day; nine until lunchtime, and then four hours' work between two o'clock and dinnertime, to suit herself.'

Just as though I'm not here, thought Suzannah

crossly. She shot him a speaking glance and met his cold eyes. 'You are agreeable to that?' he wanted to know.

It was tempting to tell him that she wasn't agreeable at all, but Lady Manbrook was still looking upset so she said in a colourless voice. 'Thank you, Professor, yes, that will do very well,' and then, because she felt peevish, 'So kind of you to bother,' she added waspishly.

'I'm not a particularly kind man,' he observed, 'but I hope that I am a just one.'

Maybe he was; he was also rude. She picked up the dance programmes and asked if the ladies would like to see them.

The next hour passed quickly, with the ladies exclaiming over the charming little cards with their coloured pencils attached by still bright cords, most of them filled by scrawled initials, one or two woefully half-empty. 'That would be Emily Wolferton,' declared Lady Manbrook. 'Such a haughty piece.' She tossed the card down and added with satisfaction, 'I always had partners,' and her sister echoed,

'And so did I.' Here's one—Phoebe's grandmother —a nasty, ill-tempered girl she was too, always wanting something she hadn't.' She looked across at the professor, sitting impassively doing nothing. 'I hope Phoebe isn't ill-tempered, Guy?'

'Oh, never, just as long as she gets what she wants,' he replied idly.

'And of course, she gets it,' observed Mrs van Beuck. 'William Davinish is too old to want any more than peace and quiet at all costs.'

He made no reply to this, but said presently,

'Perhaps Suzannah would like an hour or two to herself before dinner.' He glanced at his watch. 'I must go presently . . .'

'So soon, dear?' asked Lady Manbrook.

He looked at Suzannah. 'I'm dining with Phoebe.'

Suzannah got up, excused herself with nice manners and made for the door. The professor had it open before she reached it. He couldn't get rid of her fast enough, it seemed, but he spoke as she went past him.

'A pity we had no time to talk.'

She gave him a thoughtful look. 'Is it? I can't think of anything we would want to talk about, Professor.'

She didn't much like his smile. He said softly in a silky tone. 'You may be mouselike despite that hair of yours, but your tongue, like a mouse's tooth, is sharp.' He opened the door. 'Goodnight, Suzannah.'

She mumbled goodnight as she whisked past him.

He stood at the open door watching her disappear across the hall, and the look on his face made Lady Manbrook say, 'Such a nice girl, Guy, so neat and tidy and hard-working.'

He smiled at his aunt and wondered what Suzannah would say to that; no girl, however self-effacing, would consider that a compliment. He shrugged huge shoulders, impatient with himself for his unwilling interest. It had been easy enough to arrange this job for her with his aunts; he had done that, he reflected, out of pity and because he considered that she had been unfairly treated by Phoebe. He had no reason to feel interest in her future; he had made it possible for her to have a couple of months' respite, and in that time she could decide what she wanted to do. She would have to earn her living. He strolled back to his chair and sat for another hour or so listening to his aunts' gentle chatter.

Suzannah bounced into her little flat, fed Horace, lit the fire and got her coat, all the while muttering and grumbling to Horace, who ate his supper in a single-minded fashion and didn't bother to answer.

'He's a very rude man,' declared Suzannah. 'I think he dislikes me very much—it's most unfortunate that we had to meet again.' She tugged her coat-belt tight in a ruthless fashion, scooped up Horace and went outside. Horace, during the previous week, had indicated in a positive fashion just where he preferred to take his walk. She followed him across the yard, along the back drive and then circled the grounds of the house, which brought them to the front gates. There was never anything about at that time of the evening; Horace meandered along, stopping to savour a few blades of grass as he went. They were on the last leg of their walk, rounding the curve of the drive back to the courtyard, when the Bentley swooped silently round the corner, to brake sharply within a foot of Horace.

The professor poked his handsome head out of the car window. He said testily, 'For heaven's sake—must you stroll around in the dusk without a light? I could have killed that cat.'

However, Suzannah had Horace, shocked and indignant, clasped firmly against her. 'This,' she pointed out in a voice squeaky with fright and rage, 'is a private drive. I wasn't to know that you would come tearing round the corner at ninety miles an hour!'

He laughed. 'Thirty at the most. And I'm a good driver. But let it be a lesson to you in the future.' He withdrew his head and drove on, leaving her very cross indeed.

Safely in her room again, she looked at the clock. It was time for her to get ready for Sunday supper. She went into the tiny bathroom and began to clean her teeth. 'I hope I never see the beastly man again,' she told Horace through a mouthful of toothpaste.

The second week slid away pleasantly enough; the old ladies seemed to have taken their nephew's suggestions to heart, for she was narrowly questioned each day as to whether she had worked for longer hours than he had suggested, and when Saturday came she was told to take the day off.

Something she was glad enough to do; the dance programmes had been dealt with and neatly catalogued and she was well into the newspaper cuttings; much harder work but even more interesting, although tiring too. Besides, she had two weeks' pay in her pocket and the desire to spend some of it was very great. There wasn't enough for a dress, but she was handy with her needle; material for a skirt and wool for a sweater would leave money over for her to save. She hadn't forgotten the future; indeed, she lay awake at night sometimes worrying about it, but there was still four weeks' work, and if she limited her spending to a pair of shoes and small necessities she would have enough to tide her over until she could get another job. She would have to start looking in the situations vacant columns before she left, of course. In the meantime she settled Horace, got into her tweed suit and caught the bus into Marlborough.

She found what she wanted: a fine green wool for the skirt and green knitting wool to match it—the jumper pattern was intricate and boasted a pattern of small flowers in a number of colours—but she was a good knitter and there was time enough in her free time to work at it. She had a frugal lunch in a little café away from the main street and caught an early bus back.

Back in her flat, she lit the fire, fed Horace, and got her tea. She had brought crumpets back with her; with the curtains drawn and the lamp by the fireplace alight, she sat down contentedly munching and drinking tea. How nice the simple pleasures of life were, she observed to Horace, and licked her buttery fingers.

There was still plenty of time before dinner. She tidied away the tea things, made up the fire and spread her material on the floor and cut out her skirt. She would have to sew it by hand, but that didn't worry her; she tacked it together, tried it on in front of the small bedroom looking-glass and then got ready to go over to the house.

There was no sign of the professor during the next week, but then she hadn't expected to see him and certainly no one mentioned him. She worked away at the press cuttings, sewed her skirt in her free time and took a brisk walk each day. A dull week, but its very dullness gave her a sense of security. She went to Marlborough again on her free day, but she spent very little of her pay; the future was beginning to loom. Another three weeks and she would be finished. There were only the letters and diaries to sort and read now, and the cataloguing, now that she had made sense of the muddle, presented no difficulties. Next week, she promised herself, she would decide what was to be done. Hopefully, she would get a good reference from Lady Manbrook and a study of the domestic situations in *The Lady* seemed hopeful. She treated herself to tea in a modest café and caught the bus back.

The letters, when she began on them, were fascinating. The contents were, for the most part, innocuous enough; accounts of morning calls, tea parties and dances with descriptions of the clothes worn by the writer's friends, some of them a trifle tart. But a packet of envelopes tied with ribbon Suzannah opened with some hesitation and then tied them up again. The top letter began 'My dearest love', and to read further would have been as bad as eavesdropping. She took the bundle, and another one like it, down to the drawing-room before dinner that evening and gave them to Lady Manbrook, who looked through them, murmuring from time to time. 'Great-Aunt Alicia,' she said finally, 'and Great-Uncle Humbert—before they became engaged. How very interesting. But you did quite right to give them to me, Suzannah; if there are any more of these letters, will you fasten them together—put them into an envelope, perhaps?—and write "Private" on it. I scarcely feel that they were meant for any eyes, but those for whom they were intended. Are there many more?'

'I don't think so, Lady Manbrook, but there are several in another language—it looks a little like German . . .'

'Dutch,' said Mrs van Beuck promptly. 'Are they written or typed, my dear?'

'Typed, for the most part.'

'Marriage settlements when I married dear Everard. Dear me, such a long time ago.'

Suzannah wasn't sure what to say; she knew nothing about marriage settlements, and Mrs van Beuck was looking sad. 'We went together to the family solicitor,' she ruminated. 'I had a lovely hat—grey tulle with pink roses,' a remark which led to the two ladies talking at some length about long-forgotten toilettes. Suzannah sat between them an appreciative audience, until they went in to dinner.

It was as they drank their coffee afterwards that Lady Manbrook said, 'We shall miss you, Suzannah; you have worked so hard and I am sure you have made a splendid job of arranging those tiresome papers. Do you have any plans?'

'Not at present, Lady Manbrook. I think that I shall be finished in three weeks; the cataloguing will take a good deal of time, but I've almost finished looking through the letters and I left those until last.'

'I'm sure you will find something nice to do,' observed Mrs van Beuck comfortably. 'It must be very quiet for you here.'

'I've been very happy here, and I love the country.' Suzannah excused herself presently and went to her flat, feeling anxious. It seemed to her that the two ladies were eager for her to finish, although they hadn't said so. She sat down by the fire with Horace on her lap and studied the situations vacant column in the local paper; several pubs wanted barmaids, but even if she had known something about the work she doubted if anyone would consider her suitable; barmaids were usually pretty and buxom, and she was neither. There was a job for a home help to live in; five children in the family, must love dogs, be cheerful and prepared to assist a handicapped granny when needed; salary negotiable. Suzannah wasn't quite sure what that meant, but she had a nasty feeling that she would come off second-best in negotiations of any kind. She folded the paper tidily and decided to go to the domestic agency in Marlborough on her next day off.

It was almost the end of another week and she was sitting in the room Snow had made ready for her, carefully cataloging the last of the dance programmes, when the professor walked in.

'Still at it?' he wanted to know, and went to stand in front of the small fire, effectively cutting off its warmth.

Suzannah looked up from her work. 'Good afternoon, Professor Bowers-Bentinck,' she said pointedly, and waited for him to speak.

'If it will take the disapproving look off your face, good afternoon to you too, Suzannah. Almost finished?'

Here was another one anxious for her to be gone. She said carefully, 'Very nearly, I'm going as fast as I can . . .'

'Good. Have you another job to go to?'

'I have several likely . . .' She caught his hard blue eyes boring into her. 'Well,' she went on, 'I haven't really, but I've applied to three.'

'Any money?'

She went rather pink. 'Really, Professor, I hardly think that's your business.'

'I asked you if you had any money, Suzannah. I can see no reason why you shouldn't answer my question.'

'No, I don't suppose you can.' She drew a deep breath. 'But let me tell you something. I'm not in your employ; you were kind enough when Aunt Mabel died, although probably that was bedside manner—I imagine you can put that on and take it off again whenever you want to—but I won't be patronised . . .'

Her calm voice had become a little shrill; she took another steadying breath and added, 'If you don't mind, I'd like to get on with my work . . .'

She had been annoyed with him; she was even more annoyed now when he strolled away, closing the door gently behind him.

There was no sign of him when she joined the two old ladies in the drawing-room that evening.

'Such a pity that Guy had to go back to his consulting rooms,' observed Mrs van Beuck. 'The dear boy works far too hard; it amazes me where these people come from.' And at Suzannah's puzzled look, 'People with brain tumours, my dear. And of course dear Guy is so clever, he knows exactly what to do . . .' She drew a sharp breath. 'My dear child, I am so sorry, for the moment I forgot that your aunt . . .'

Suzannah said composedly, 'It's quite all right, Mrs van Bueck, there was nothing to be done for my aunt; Professor Bowers-Bentinck examined her most carefully and was kindness itself.'

Quite a different man to the visitor she had had that afternoon. She supposed that she must annoy him in some way, certainly he needled her into being rude. Aunt Mabel would have been vexed; so, too, would her two companions if they could hear her!

She sat listening with half an ear to the two ladies' gentle chatter. 'I cannot believe that the dear boy will be thirty-five next week,' observed Lady Manbrook. 'It seems only the other day he and his dear parents were here on a visit—while he was at Marlborough, was it not? Such a pity they haven't lived to see him achieve fame in the medical world. And so modest, too; never an unkind word.'

Obviously, thought Suzannah, there was a side to the professor which she had failed to discover.

And not likely to either; another week went by with no sign of him—and why should there be? she argued to herself. He was a busy man and his work kept him in London. She was almost at the end of her cataloguing by now; another four or five days and she would be finished. She was too honest to spin it out for a few more days, but she was sorely tempted, for she had had no replies to the advertisments she had answered.

She resisted the temptation, arranged the last of the letters in a neat pile beside everything else and went to tell Lady Manbrook that four more days' work would suffice to tidy everything away once more.

That lady looked surprised. 'Already, my dear? How very quick you have been. You will need a day or so to clear up your own things, of course, and make arrangements. Croft will drive you back . . .' She paused. 'Where to, Suzannah? Is not someone living in your former home?'

'Mrs Coffin will give me a room until I go to another job, Lady Manbrook.'

'Ah, yes, of course. I'm sure you must be much in demand.'

Suzannah hoped that she would be, too. But the last day came with nothing in the post for her, so she stowed Horace in his basket, packed the geranium carefully, wished the two old ladies goodbye, made her farewells in the kitchen and then got into the car beside Croft. Mrs Coffin had sent her a cheerful letter, happily agreeing to let her have a room for as long as she would need one; all the same, Suzannah's heart sank as Croft drove her away from what had seemed to her to be a haven of security. True, she had saved almost all her wages, but they weren't going to go far . . .

Mrs Coffin welcomed her with genuine pleasure, and over high tea, eaten after the shop was closed for the day, listened with sympathy to Suzannah's doubts about the future.

'Don't worry, love,' she said in her comfortable voice, 'something'll turn up, and you're welcome to stay here just as long as you want to.'

She patted Suzannah's hand over the table and went on, 'Now tell me all about your job? Was it interesting? Did you meet anyone nice?'

She meant young men, of course. 'No, but I'll tell you who I met, and I was surprised. That professor who came to see Aunt Mabel when she was so ill . . .' Her voice faltered for a moment. 'He's Lady Manbrook's nephew or something.'

'That was nice, dear . . .'

'Not really. He doesn't like me, you know, and he asked a lot of questions!'

'Did he, now? I do hear from the housekeeper at the manor that Miss Phoebe's in a rare bad temper these days. Everyone thought that the professor was going to marry her; she boasted about it too, but I met Mr Toms the other day and he said that he'd heard her telling some friend or other that she hadn't seen him in weeks. Don't know much about him myself, but he was always very civil to me and Dr Warren sets great store by him. I shouldn't think he'd put up with Miss Phoebe's nasty tempers.'

Suzannah wondered silently if he had a nasty temper too; she thought it quite likely. A man who liked his own way, she felt sure.

It was pleasant to be back in the village again, although she didn't go near her old home. Indeed, she spent a good part of each day writing replies to the advertisements Mrs Coffin obligingly allowed her to look for in the papers and magazines which she sold. After three days she had two replies, both of them quite obdurate about pets. To leave him behind was impossible; Mrs Coffin liked him well enough, but she had a cat and a very elderly dog of her own, and although they tolerated Horace as a temporary lodger, there would be no question of him settling down with them.

Suzannah had taken over the cooking and some of the household chores from her kind landlady, anxious not to be too much of a burden to her, and each afternoon, after they had eaten their midday dinner, she took over the shop too while Mrs Coffin had what she called 'a bit of a lie down'. It was on the fourth day of her stay that Professor Bowers-Bentinck walked in.

She was adding up the items that Mrs Batch, from the other end of the village, had bought and, since Mrs Coffin didn't believe in new-fangled things like electric cash registers but wrote everything down on a bit of paper, any that came in handy, Suzannah was totting up her sums on the outside wrapper of the best back bacon she had just sliced.

The doorbell jangled as he went in and she looked up briefly, muttering, 'One pound fifty-three . . .' and then, at the sight of him, forgot how far she had got to.

She said vexedly, 'Oh, look what you've made me do—now I'll have to start again.' Which she did, adding her sums twice to make sure before giving Mrs Batch the total.

That lady knew the professor by sight, of course, she bade him good afternoon now, hoped he was well, remarked upon the weather and handed Suzannah a five-pound note.

Suzannah counted out the change, put her customer's purchases in her plastic carrier bag, and wished her good day, and when she had gone turned her attention to the professor.

'Good afternoon. Do you wish to buy something?'

He looked faintly surprised. 'Er—no. Have you taken over the shop from Mrs Coffin?'

'No but while I'm here I mind it for her while she has a short rest.'

'So you have no job?'

She didn't answer that at once, then she said briefly, 'No, not yet.'

'Then may I put a proposition to you and hope that you will overlook your dislike of me sufficiently to listen to it?'

'You don't like me either,' said Suzannah matter-of-factly.

He looked down his commanding nose at her. 'I am not aware that I have any feelings about you, good or bad, Suzannah.' He smiled thinly. 'Now, if you would listen to me and not interrupt.'

A high-handed remark which left her conveniently without words.

The professor pushed aside a basket of assorted biscuits, several tins of soup and a large card announcing that there would be a whist drive in the village hall next Wednesday, and sat down at the edge of the counter. He took up a great deal of room, and Suzannah had to look up to see his face, which rather annoyed her.

'I have a patient,' he informed her, 'who has

recovered from a cerebral tumour which I removed some weeks ago. She is fit to return to her home—in Holland, I should add—but she needs a sensible companion with plenty of common sense to remain with her until she feels able to resume a normal life. She refuses to have a nurse, and quite rightly; she is no longer in need of nursing care, but she needs someone reliable to depend upon who, at the same time, will remain in the background unless she is needed. I believe that you would be absolutely right for the job.'

'You put it very clearly,' said Suzannah, digesting this opinion of herself. So she was just right to sit meekly in the background, was she, waiting until she was wanted? I'd like to show him, she thought, fiercely, I'd like just one chance to dine at the Ritz with a duke wearing black tulle and diamonds and cut this wretch dead when he saw me there . . .

'Suzannah,' the doctor's voice was compelling, 'you are allowing your thoughts to wander. I trust you have understood me?'

'For how long?' she asked briskly, and, 'What would my salary be?'

He gave her an intent look. 'A few weeks at the most. The salary is adequate.' He mentioned a sum which seemed to her to be excessive.

She said, 'Isn't that rather a lot of money to pay someone to sit in the background, even if she is reliable and dependable and—what was the other virtue?—sensible?'

He said with scarcely veiled impatience, 'Oh, I'm sorry, I explained rather badly; I intended nothing personal.'

She said kindly, 'No, I don't expect you did, but

you should be more careful you know, especially when you are talking to girls like me.'

'Why?'

'Well, just think for yourself, Professor: I'm no beauty, I've no money, no job and the future's a bit vague; I don't want to be reminded of any of those things. But it was kind of you to ask me, only of course I can't . . .'

'Why not?'

'Horace. He can't stay here with Mrs Coffin; she has a cat and a dog already and they put up with him, but only for the moment. No one else would want him.'

Professor Bowers-Bentinck was surprised to hear himself say, 'He can come to my home. I have a housekeeper who I know will welcome him and take good care of him.'

'Would she? He might escape . . .'

'There is a garden-room behind the house where he can roam without going outside. I assure you that I will be responsible for his safety.'

She was surprised to find that she believed him when he said that; he might be a disagreeable man, at least towards her, but she felt that he was a man of his word. She nodded her neat head. 'Very well, I'd be glad of the job; if I can save enough money I thought I might train as a nurse or a nanny . . .'

'And Horace?' he wanted to know.

'Oh, that's why I must save some money first, so that I can find a little flat or a room and live out.'

He stood up then and said with a return of his impatience, 'Have you any idea of the high rent you would have to pay?'

'Oh, yes, but I'd go to one of the provincial hospitals—Yeovil or Salisbury, somewhere like that.' She was aware that he was no longer interested; he had got what he had come for and her future was no concern of his.

'Will you let me know when I am to start work—I've no passport . . .'

He was at the door. 'You will get all the details in a letter. Send for a passport at once—better still, fill in the form and send it to me—I'll forward it with a note asking for the matter to be treated urgently.'

'Where shall I send it?'

'To Elliot's Hospital, London. Mark it personal and urgent.' He nodded a casual goodbye and closed the door quietly behind him, leaving her to wonder if she had dreamt the lot.

Mrs Coffin, when appraised of the afternoon's happenings, crowed with delight, assured her that her fortune was made and produced an application form for a passport from under the post office counter. 'You fill that in now, love,' she urged, 'and post it this very day. You can run across to the doctor's and the vicar's and get them to sign it for you. Get photos in Marlborough for it from the post office and send them off.'

She spent the rest of the day speculating as to the exact nature of the job Suzannah had accepted. 'Perhaps it's someone rich,' she observed, 'or a titled lady, living in Holland, too—let's hope you'll be able to understand her.' She glanced at Suzannah. 'You'll need some clothes, dearie.'

Suzannah supposed that even a faceless person sitting in the background would need to be decently clad. She had the new skirt, of course, and the sweater was half knitted. Her suit would have to do, but she would need a couple of blouses and another sweater and a decent dress besides.

'I'll have to buy one, there might not be time to make it,' she said out loud.

She was quite right, there was a letter for her the next day, giving the name of the patient, a Juffrouw Julie van Dijl, twenty-two years old, whose home was in the Hague. Unmarried, with parents and two brothers. There followed details of her condition and a veiled warning that she might be prone to short bouts of ill-temper and depression.

'Aren't we all?' muttered Suzannah, reading the businesslike typing.

But the salary was written there clearly to be seen, and so were the conditions of her job; two hours to herself each day and a free day each week, though she must be prepared to be at her employer's beck and call at all hours, which seemed a bit ominous. But the money was generous and would make all the difference to her future.

She got the next but to Marlborough and enriched her wardrobe with two blouses, a thin sweater, some underwear and a very plain silk jersey dress in pewter-grey. Well-satisfied, she returned to Mrs Coffin's and spent the next two days knitting like one of the furies, uncertain as to how long she would have before being summoned. The letter had ended with a curt request for her to be prepared to start work at short notice, so she packed the best of her clothes under the eye of a suspicious Horace and washed her hair and possessed her soul in patience.

She didn't have long to wait. Her passport arrived several days later; the professor must have a member of his family or a close friend at the passport office, she decided. And two days later there was another letter, requesting her in impersonal type to hold herself ready to leave in two days' time. She would be taken to London by car, Horace would be deposited as agreed and she would then join the lady she was to accompany. It was signed by the professor, his signature strongly resembling a spider in its death throes.

The driver of the car, when it arrived, proved to be a fatherly man, very spruce but certainly not a chauffeur. He introduced himself as Cobb, stowed her luggage in the boot, arranged Horace in his basket on the back seat and held the door open for her.

Suzannah gave Mrs Coffin a last hug and then asked to sit in front with him; he looked kind and perhaps he would give her some information about the professor.

In this she was mistaken; Cobb was kind, chatty as well, but not one word did he let drop about the professor other than to say that he was employed by him. So Suzannah passed the journey to town in trivial conversation, alternately feeling excited and apprehensive.

They had left early in the day and the morning rush was over by the time they reached London; all the same, it took a little time for Cobb to arrive at their destination: a quiet backwater of a street, tucked away behind Harley Street, lined with tall, splendidly maintained houses gleaming with paintwork, their brass door-knockers glistening with daily polishing. Cobb drew to a gentle halt before one of these houses, got out, opened the door and reached for Horace, and by the time he had done this the front door had been opened by a cosy-looking woman of middle age, dressed very neatly in black. She smiled at Suzannah as she mounted the few steps to the door.

'Good morning, miss. I'm Mrs Cobb, housekeeper to the professor. I'm to see that you have a cup of coffee before you leave, and I'll show you where your cat will live. Glad to have him, too; the professor's got a dog, but my old cat, Flossie, died a while ago and I do miss her.'

She had led the way into the house as she spoke, into a small hall, very elegant with its striped walls and polished floor. 'If you wouldn't mind coming to the kitchen, miss . . .'

There was a baize door beside the curving staircase at the back of the hall; they went through it, down some steps and through another door into the kitchen. The house, Suzannah realised, was a good deal larger than it appeared from the street, for the kitchen was large with a glimpse of smaller rooms leading from it and, through the window at the end, quite a long garden.

'He'll live here with me,' explained Mrs Cobb, 'but of course he'll have the run of the house, and through this door . . .' she opened another door and went down a short passage which in turn opened into a garden-room, 'there's all this for him to roam in. And be sure I'll take the greatest deal of care of him, miss. If you let him out so that he can look around . . . ?'

The sun warmed the garden-room, and it was comfortably furnished with lounge chairs and little tables. 'You just have your coffee here,' advised Mrs

Cobb, 'and let the little man roam.'

She bustled off and Horace, freed from his basket, sauntered around, sniffing at the greenery and finally settling in one of the chairs. Mrs Cobb, coming back with the coffee-tray, looked pleased. 'There! I knew he'd settle. Handsome, isn't he?'

Suzannah sat and drank her coffee and then, warned by Mrs Cobb that Cobb would be driving her to her employer in ten minutes' time, went away to tidy herself in the luxurious little cloakroom tucked away behind the staircase. From the glimpse she had of the house, the professor lived in the greatest comfort—more luxury. She would have liked to have seen more of the house. There were several doors leading from the hall, but they were all shut, and she resisted the temptation to open them and went back to the garden-room to say goodbye to Horace, who, curled up half asleep, did no more than open an eye.

'I'll be back,' she assured him, and followed Mrs Cobb back into the hall once more and then out to the car. She felt terrible: like someone who had jumped into the deep end of a swimming pool and remembered at the last moment that she couldn't swim.

CHAPTER FOUR

THEY hadn't far to go, but during the short drive Cobb, seeing her downcast face, talked cheerfully. 'The missus will love Horace,' he told her. 'Dotes on cats, she does. I dare say she'll drop you a line to let you know how he is.'

Suzannah said gratefully, 'Oh, do you suppose she would? I'd be very grateful; you see, I'm not quite sure how long I'll be away.' She added doubtfully, 'I hope I'll do.'

'Don't you fret, miss. The professor doesn't make mistakes; if he thought you were right for the job, then you'll be OK.'

He turned the car into a Belgravia square. 'Here we are.' He drew in his breath with a satisfied hiss. 'Just on time, too.'

The Bentley was gliding to a halt before one of the massive houses in the square, and Cobb drew up just behind it, got out, opened Suzannah's door and with a cheerful, 'Goodbye, miss,' left her with the professor, who had got out of his car too.

His, 'Good morning,' was curt but not unfriendly. 'I'll introduce you to Juffrouw van Dijl; you will leave with her in her car in about half an hour. Did Cobb give you an envelope?'

'Yes, I've not opened it.'

'Do so when you have the opportunity.' He didn't say what was in it, but led the way through the imposing front door, held open by an impassive man-servant. 'I have no time to waste, so don't dawdle,' he advised her unnecessarily.

They were led up a grand staircase to a room over-looking the street, furnished in an opulent style which Suzannah found overpowering and in which were a number of people: an elderly man, a slightly younger woman, a youngish man whose eyes were too close together and a very pretty girl with dark hair and eyes, dressed dramatically in the very height of fashion and looking nervous and excited.

When she saw the professor she rushed to meet him and caught him by the arm. 'Guy—are you sure I'll be all right? You will come and see me? What will I do if I feel ill?'

He said gently, 'Why should you feel ill, Julie? You were always a remarkably healthy girl, and now that you are well again there is no reason why you should be anything else. Besides, I have brought Suzannah with me; she will keep an eye on you—and she is not a nurse, you know, just someone to keep you company and remind you from time to time that you're perfectly well again.'

The girl looked at Suzannah, taking in her neat, unfashionable appearance. 'Oh, hello.'

She nodded carelessly, not listening to Suzannah's polite, 'How do you do, Miss van Dijl?' and turned back to the professor.

'You will come, won't you, soon?'

'When I can arrange it, Julie. I'm tied up at the moment.' He left her and crossed the room to shake hands with the older man and woman and introduced Suzannah. 'Mr and Mrs South,' he told her, 'are aunt and uncle to Juffrouw van Dijl; she has been staying for a few days with them before returning home.'

Suzannah shook hands with them and wondered just where home was. Just as though he had read her thoughts, the professor said quietly, 'You will find all the information you need in the envelope, Suzannah.'

He went away presently, and shortly after that Suzannah accompanied her new employer out to the Rolls-Royce outside and got in beside her. Her luggage had been put in the boot, together with a great many cases belonging to Juffrouw van Dijl arranged there, and she sat quietly while tearful farewells were exchanged. No one had thought to bid her goodbye; she didn't mind that the aunt and uncle had overlooked her, but she chalked up another black mark against the professor for doing no more than nodding at her as he left. It had been a last-minute, absent-minded nod, too, as though he had remembered just in time that she was there.

The young man had stayed in the background; now he put his head through the open window of the car and spoke urgently to Juffrouw van Dijl; Suzannah tried not to listen but it wouldn't have mattered if she had for he spoke in some language she couldn't understand —Dutch, she thought—and her companion had answered just as urgently before they drove off.

They were going by hovercraft to Holland, and the drive to Dover took no more than an hour and a half. Juffrouw van Dijl made no attempt at conversation but sat, wrapped in thought, ignoring Suzannah, so that after a while she took out the envelope she had been given and read its contents: a detailed resumé of everything she needed to know while she was in Holland.

More information as to Juffrouw van Dijl's way of life, a reiteration of the hours she was to work and when she was to be free, the arrangement made to pay her salary each week, the currency, the name and telephone number of the family doctor, where she should go if she needed help . . .

Why should I need help? wondered Suzannah, and decided that was the professor covering all risks. There was even a short paragraph suggesting suitable dressing for the evening and the name of a bank where she might wish to deposit her money. All very helpful, she decided, folding away the letter carefully and tucking it into a pocket.

Their journey was uneventful, the chauffeur saw to everything and Suzannah had nothing more to do than follow her companion on to the hovercraft. Once on land again, they waited while the car was unloaded and then got into its comfort once again. Suzannah was surprised when Juffrouw van Dijl spoke. 'This is my father's car. He sent Jan the chauffeur to bring me home; I am not in the habit of travelling without a servant.' She paused. 'I suppose you know that I have been dangerously ill?'

'Yes, Professor Bowers-Bentinck has explained everything to me.'

'Good, it is tiresome having to tell people what has to be done. He told me that you aren't a nurse—I never wish to see another as long as I live.'

Which seemed a bit ungrateful to Suzannah, although she didn't say so.

Her companion went on, 'You are, of course, here to make yourself useful. You won't put yourself forward, I hope. It is only because Professor Bowers-Bentinck insisted that I should have someone sensible to be with me that I consented to employ you.'

Suzannah opened her mouth to answer this and then shut it again; she was quite sure that she wouldn't like the job. She certainly hadn't taken to Juffrouw van Dijl, but the salary was good, and according to the professor it would only be for a few weeks. Besides, she had every intention of letting him see that she was capable of coping with his patient; he must have known that she was self-willed and spoilt . . .

As she didn't answer, Juffrouw van Dijl turned to look at her. 'There is one thing I find agreeable about you,' she conceded. 'You don't answer back or chatter.'

A remark which Suzannah greeted with a faint smile and a well-modulated word of thanks.

Juffrouw van Dijl seemed disposed to talk. 'Of course, Professor Bowers-Bentinck is my surgeon, but he is also a very old friend of my family—we have been close for many years. I have not quite decided if I wish to marry him; for some time it was thought that he would marry some girl in Wiltshire, I believe, the niece of an English friend he had known for some time, but he sees her no longer and perhaps I shall decide to marry him, after all.'

Suzannah murmured and wondered what the professor would have to say to that. The girl in Wiltshire would be Phoebe, and she wondered why he was no longer interested in her. He could, she supposed, pick and choose among his women acquaintances; he was good-looking and successful and presumably, from what she had seen of his home, comfortably endowed with the world's goods. Perhaps he was content with his life as it was; he might even be hiding a broken heart behind that bland face of his. It seemed unlikely. On the whole, she reflected, it would be a pity if he were to marry the girl beside her; she didn't seem very suitable, but perhaps she was being unfair; she had been very ill and it must have cost her a great effort to get well again, even with the aid of the professor's surgery. She warmed towards her companion and said impulsively, 'I'm sure you will both be very happy,' not at all sure that it would turn out like that. Her warmth was wasted.

'I didn't ask for your comments,' said Juffrouw van Dijl sharply. 'Kindly keep your opinions to yourself in future.'

A future, thought Suzannah to herself, which wouldn't last too long if she could help it.

She looked out at the countryside; it looked flat, very green and rather uninteresting, but she reminded herself that this was only a very small part of Holland. Beyond the big cities there would be villages and trees and lakes. Perhaps she would get a chance to see them before she returned to England; it was such a small country, she would be able to see a good deal in a couple of days. She occupied herself with these pleasant thoughts until the Hague was reached and she turned her attention to her surroundings. It seemed a pleasant city and some of the old buildings looked interesting, but they passed them by and drove to the more modern sector of the city, turning away presently into a wide avenue, tree-lined, with large houses on either side. Into the gates of one of these the chauffeur turned the car, stopping on a sweep so pristine that it must have been combed hourly, and getting out to open the car doors. Suzannah nipped out on her own while he assisted

Juffrouw van Dijl to alight, which gave her time to take a look around. She was disappointed: the house, built at the turn of the century, was ugly. It was of red brick, very large and hung around with a great number of balconies, and at each corner of its elaborate roof there were small turrets.

'Lookout posts?' Suzannah asked herself, craning her neck. 'But what is there to see in such a respectable neighbourhood?'

There was no one to answer her; following Juffrouw van Dijl's footsteps, she mounted the flight of stairs which swept grandly to the vast mahogany door and wondered what it would be like inside.

The door, opened by a man who murmured a welcome in a colourless voice, revealed a large hall, papered in crimson and hung with stuffed animals' heads, arranged in patterns between displays of nasty-looking spears and swords. She averted her eyes and trod across a vast expanse of Turkish carpet at the heels of Juffrouw van Dijl, to enter a room at one side of the hall. It was as overpowering as the hall, only this time the wallpaper was dark green, embossed and almost covered by paintings framed inches-deep in gilt. The furniture was large, solid and beautifully polished and there was too much of it—tables loaded with reading-lamps, silver-framed photos, china figurines and the like.

The lady who came to greet them was quite dwarfed by her surroundings; she was quite small, although stout, with a sweet expression on her face and an air of timidity. Surely not Juffrouw van Dijl's mother? wondered Suzannah. But it was; the little lady embraced her daughter with a good deal of emotion, begged her to sit down and not exert herself and looked at Suzannah. 'You must be the young lady who is to care for my daughter,' she declared in fluent, accented English. 'Such a relief to me, for I am not at all sure how much Julie may do. Professor Bowers-Bentinck did explain to me, but I am quite stupid about such things; that is why he suggested that a good, sensible girl might relieve me of worry.'

Suzannah shook hands and murmured appropriately; so many people had considered her sensible that she was beginning to believe it.

A maid had come in with a coffee-tray and Mevrouw van Dijl busied herself pouring it out while her daughter sat languidly, making monosyllabic replies to her anxious questions. Presently, with a word of apology, they reverted to Dutch and Suzannah sat drinking her coffee, listening to the meaningless words. She understood none of it, but it was plain then that Juffrouw van Dijl was laying down the law to her mother, who nodded her head meekly and presently turned to Suzannah.

'Julie is anxious to visit all her friends and continue with her old life,' she announced worriedly, 'but I think that is something the professor might not like. Did he say anything . . . ?'

Suzannah, who had an excellent memory, quoted the parts of the letter which she felt could be mentioned harmlessly. 'He was most anxious that Juffrouw van Dijl should live quietly for at least two weeks; a few friends, but not any parties or dancing, and early nights with a rest after lunch each day. And she is never to go anywhere on her own, at least until he has seen her again.'

'You heard that, *lieveling*? It is hard, I know, but we will make it up to you as soon as we may do so. You have been so ill, and another week or two will restore you completely.'

Juffrouw van Dijl said something fierce in Dutch and turned to Suzannah. 'And suppose I refuse all this silly cosseting?'

'Professor Bowers-Bentinck has instructed me to tell him immediately if his instructions aren't carried out.'

Julie van Dijl tossed her lovely head. 'Oh, he did, did he?' She smiled. 'Dear Guy, he wishes me to get well quickly, so I will do as he says. But you will not stay a day longer than is necessary. I will put up with you because he wishes it, but only because of that. You had better go to your room and unpack . . .'

'Thank you, but first I must make sure that you go to your room too and rest. Do you wish me to unpack for you?'

'Certainly not. I have a maid. And I am not tired . . .'

Suzannah said in her calm voice, 'Perhaps not, but you have just said that you would do as the professor asked.'

Juffrouw van Dijl made a face and got up out of her chair, and her mother gave a relieved smile. 'We shall see you later, Julie. I'm sure Professor Bowers-Bentinck knows best, he is one of the most successful surgeons there is and he is, after all, a family friend.'

Her daughter gave her an impatient look, not speaking, and strolled out of the room with Suzannah trailing her.

The man who had opened the door was in the hall and with him a tall, bony woman, who exclaimed with pleasure at the sight of Juffrouw van Dijl and hurried her up the solid staircase. Half-way to the floor above, she turned and beckoned to Suzannah, who had been wondering what she should do. The man, some kind of butler she imagined, had ignored her and she didn't think she was supposed to go back to Mevrouw van Dijl. She went upstairs thankfully and crossed the wide landing to where the other two were waiting for her.

Julie van Dijl's room was a splendid one, overlooking the side of the house; it would have been a fitting background for a film star with its lush carpet, satin curtains and canopied bed. Suzannah stood uncertainly on its threshold.

'You have the room next to mine, through that door.'

So she crossed the room and opened another door. The room beyond was very much smaller, nicely furnished but impersonal, rather like a hotel-room. But the view from the window was pleasant as it overlooked the garden too. Suzannah took off her jacket, peeped round another door leading to a small bathroom and went back to Julie's room.

She was surprised when she said, 'Your room's all right? The nurse was there when I was ill.' She was still more surprised when Julie added in an almost friendly voice, 'I like the door to be kept open at night.' She hesitated. 'In case I should want anything.'

'Of course. Can I do anything to help you now?'

The maid was unpacking at the other end of the room, her head bent over the piles of clothes she was folding carefully.

'I think that I am now tired. I shall lie down.' A signal for Suzannah to take the soft quilt from the day-bed by the window and spread it out invitingly. She plumped up the pillows too, and then tucked her charge in without fuss. 'A book to read?' she asked.

'No, you had better unpack. I suppose you want tea.'
She said something to the maid, who went away,
annoyed at being hindered from her unpacking. 'We
dine at seven o'clock—much earlier than in England—
Anna will help me change. I suppose you have
something fit to wear?'

Suzannah reminded herself that Julie van Dijl had
been very ill. 'I have a dress,' she said calmly. 'I hadn't
expected to take my meals with your family.'

Her companion said peevishly, 'Professor Bowers-
Bentinck said that it was correct for you to do so.' She
made an impatient sound. 'I am like a bear on a chain.'

'No', said Suzannah gently, 'you are someone who
has made a miraculous recovery and needs to be
cherished until you are quite well and strong again.'

Julie van Dijl said pettishly, 'How good you sound—
a little prig . . .'

'I really don't know. I've never been quite sure what
a prig was. But I have the professor's instructions and I
shall do my best to carry them out.'

In her room she unpacked, drank the tea which had
been brought, and took herself off to the bathroom
where she lay for a long time in the blissfully hot water
and thought about the weeks ahead of her. They
weren't going to be easy . . .

Julie's father was at dinner, a stout, middle-aged
man who had very little to say, although he was kind
enough to Suzannah, but he left the talk to his wife and
daughter and it was Julie who dominated the conversation. Naturally enough, it was mostly of herself and her
stay in London and the hospital; she had little to say
that was good about that. The fact that the professor

had saved her life, aided by the skill of the nursing staff, seemed to have evaded her—probably she had been too ill to realise the care she had received. She enlarged at length about the awful food, and the fact that, even in a private room, she had not been allowed visitors for weeks. Her parents had been there, of course, but she didn't count them. 'All my friends,' she complained, 'coming to cheer me up, and that awful dragon of a sister sending them away.'

'But now you are back home, *lieveling*,' her mother pointed out, 'and almost your old self.'

She had smiled across the table at Suzannah as she spoke, wordlessly apologising for her daughter's criticism. 'I am sure that Guy will find a great improvement when he comes to see you.'

'Well, I intend to have some fun before then, Mama.' Julie shot a defiant look at Suzannah, who pretended not to see it. The salary was a most generous one; she began to see why.

The first few days passed tolerably well; various friends came to see Julie, and her wardrobe was combed through and pronounced unwearable, but she showed no desire to go anywhere or do anything other than lounge around in her room, reading magazines and chatting with her friends. Suzannah coaxed her to take a short walk each day and saw her firmly into her bed each evening. The worst part was getting her to rest after lunch, something which was only achieved after a stormy tussle ending for the most part in tears. But once tucked up on her day-bed with a novel or magazine she slept within minutes, leaving Suzannah free to take her few hours of freedom.

She didn't dare go too far. She had begged a street

map from the butler, who, sour though he might look, was helpful, and set about exploring the neighbouring streets so that within a few days she had a good idea of where she was; ten minutes' brisk walk from the Scheveningseweg, the main road between den Haag and Scheveningen. There were parks to the left and right of the road, and trams trundling past every few minutes as well as buses. On her day off it would be an easy matter to get into the heart of the city. She looked forward to this; she realised after the first few evenings that a second dress was essential. Indeed, Juffrouw van Dijl had remarked tartly that when they had guests for dinner she would have to wear something more suitable. 'Even if you are in the background,' she pointed out, 'you can't look like a shop girl.'

Suzannah took her tongue between her teeth while rage bubbled. She said lightly, 'I should imagine that shop girls dress a good deal better than I. As soon as I have a free day I'll go shopping; something dark and very plain.'

Julie had looked at her suspiciously, wondering if she had meant it. 'But your hair,' she complained. 'It is so red . . .'

'Yes, isn't it? But don't ask me to dye it, because that's something I will not do.'

But before she had her day off Julie decided that she had to go shopping. 'You'll come with me, of course,' she said. 'I haven't anything fit to wear. There are several boutiques I go to, and we can stay in town for lunch.'

Suzannah made no demur; for one thing it wouldn't have been of much use, and for another, according to the letter of instructions she anxiously re-read each evening, Julie was to lead a normal life if she wished, provided she rested, went to bed at a reasonable hour and didn't tire herself.

Easier said than done, reflected Suzannah, but Julie showed no signs of tiredness, nor did she complain of headaches. Suzannah kept a brief record of each day and its happenings, for she felt sure that when the professor did come he would require her to give a detailed account of his patient's activities.

The day's shopping left Julie van Dijl more or less satisfied and Suzannah frankly envious. They had been driven to the heart of den Haag and deposited in Lange Voorhout, where a number of exclusive boutiques rubbed elegant shoulders. Julie van Dijl appeared to be a well-known client with them all: dresses and suits and ballgowns were displayed in a seemingly unending flow of colour and fabric while she chose what she liked without—as far as Suzannah could see—once asking the price. They sat on little gilt chairs and drank delicious coffee, and after a time Suzannah, sitting just behind Julie, ignored by everyone and not minding at all, began playing a kind of game with herself, deciding which of the outfits she would buy if she were in Julie's shoes.

They lunched in Le Baron restaurant at the Hotel des Indes, a stone's throw from the boutiques they had been visiting, and over the meal Julie van Dijl became quite friendly.

'I shall have that gold tissue dress with the roses,' she observed, 'and the pink satin with the tulle stole. I shall need at least two suits, and I liked the satin blouses with them . . . That grey knitted three-piece was quite nice, but the colour's wrong.' She paused to glance at

Suzannah's bright head. 'Right for you though, but of course you would never wear anything like that. I dare say you shop at Marks and Spencer.'

Suzannah said without heat, 'Yes, when I can afford to.' A remark which left her companion without words for a few moments.

'What will you do when you leave here?'

'I have no idea at the moment, but there is always a job, you know—mother's help or domestic work . . .'

Julie said slowly, 'Guy—Professor Bowers-Bentinck told my mother that you were to have gone to a university. I suppose you are clever.'

'Oh, no. The best I could hope for was a degree in English so that I could get a teacher's post . . .' She paused because Julie had gone off into peals of laughter.

'But you don't look like a schoolteacher. Did you wish to be one?'

'Not particularly; it was a way of earning a living.'

Julie looked at her in astonishment. 'But if you do not wish to work, why do you not marry?'

'No one has asked me,' said Suzannah. The mildness of her voice belied the temper swelling inside her. 'Do you want to see if you can find anything instead of the three piece you don't like?'

There was one more boutique which Julie declared might have something to suit her, and happily she found what she was looking for there; just in time to walk the length of Lange Voorhout and find the car waiting for them.

Julie, content with her shopping, was easily persuaded to go to bed early and have her dinner there on a tray, which left Suzannah and Mevrouw van Dijl to dine together. At first the conversation was rather stilted, but presently Mevrouw van Dijl began to talk about her daughter. 'She is spoilt,' she said with an air of apology, 'but her father is so often away from home, and when he returns there is nothing he will not do for her, and of course she never listens to me. Her two brothers are both away, but they spoil her as well.' The good lady sighed. 'She needs a husband . . . there was someone, but he is in the diplomatic service and was posted to Shanghai—or was it Hong Kong? Anyway, too far . . .'

'He'll come back,' comforted Suzannah, 'I mean, they only stay in one place for a few years, don't they?' She frowned in thought. 'And surely they get leave?'

'Julie made me promise not to tell him about her— her disability.'

'But it's not a disability,' said Suzannah strongly. 'It was a tumour which Professor Bowers-Bentinck removed and she is completely cured.'

'Yes,' agreed her companion doubtfully, 'so we have been assured. Julie is very—how do you say?— enamoured of him.'

'Well, that's only natural, isn't it? He saved her life; besides he's very good looking and I dare say charming to her. But that won't last, at least, if she loves this other man, it won't.'

'You are a sensible girl,' observed Mevrouw van Dijl. 'Julie is a dear girl, but she is used to having her own way. You are not unhappy with us?'

'Certainly not, Mevrouw. Julie is making a splendid recovery. I'm sure Professor Bowers-Bentinck will be delighted with her progress.'

Which wasn't quite true; not that she was unhappy, but her days were filled with small pinpricks, some of them intentional. Alone with Julie she was treated almost—though not quite—as a friend, but when Julie's friends came to see her or she went to see them, Suzannah was ignored or treated with a careless indifference which she found hard to bear. She had been warned that she would expect to remain in the background and she hadn't expected anything else, but to be delegated there with an, 'And you can make yourself scarce, Suzannah,' or, what was worse, 'Go away until I ring for you,' was lowering.

But she was treated with courtesy by Julie's parents and the servants, and she began to wonder if Julie was being deliberately ill mannered for some reason of her own. There was nothing to be done about it; she had accepted the job and the professor had told her that Julie was unpredictable at times.

She felt much better about it when at the end of the week she found an envelope in her room with her first week's wages. Moreover, she was to have a free day on the morrow. She accompanied Julie to a friend's house that morning and gave no sign of rancour when she was told casually to make herself scarce for an hour. She didn't go far, of course; she was there to keep an eye on her charge, which meant keeping out of sight but never so distant that she couldn't be summoned in a moment. She went and sat outside in the rather chilly autumn morning, listening to the murmur of voices and laughter from the drawing-room behind her.

Armed with her pay packet, she took a tram to the city centre on the next day; Julie was to spend the day with her parents at an aunt's house in the country and Suzannah, freed from her duties, spent a blissful few hours roaming round the shops. The grey jersey dress was no longer adequate; she had worn it each evening and was only too aware of the faintly mocking look which Julie cast at it. Boutiques were out of the question; she roamed C & A and then de Bijenkorf—rather more pricey, but she liked the clothes there.

The pretty dresses there were tempting, but she had to bear in mind that since she must keep in the background, something unassuming was called for. She found it presently—a soft grey-blue crêpe, long-sleeved with a discreet neckline, a mid-calf skirt and nothing about it to date it for a year or two. It was within her means, too; she found a coffee shop and made a frugal lunch in a glow of satisfaction.

She wore it that evening at dinner and Mevrouw van Dijl said kindly, 'That's a pretty dress, Suzannah, I like the colour,' so that she smiled with a pleasure which refused to be damped by Julie's rude,

'Spent all your money, Suzannah? Why don't you buy something pretty?'

Which made Suzannah wonder why she stayed to put up with such rudeness, even making allowances for Julie's recent illness. But the professor had said that the girl needed someone with her, although Julie had shown no signs of the depression he had mentioned. There had been plenty of ill temper, though!

Some of Julie's young friends had come in after dinner and stayed rather late, and by the time that Suzannah had made sure that Julie was in bed and half asleep it was well past midnight. She curled up in her own bed and closed her eyes and slept at once.

She wasn't sure what had wakened her. She sat up in bed to listen and then got out of bed; Julie was muttering and moaning softly. Suzannah went into her room and saw by the light of the bedside lamp that she was asleep but restless. As she reached the bed, Julie started up and burst into tears. 'Suzannah, don't go. I've had a dream—I'm not ill again, am I? I feel awful—I'm not going to die? Guy said I'd been cured, but perhaps he was only saying that . . .'

Suzannah sat on the side of the bed and put an arm round the girl.

'I'm quite sure that the professor wouldn't tell you something that wasn't true. He said you were cured, so you can take it that you are. You're not ill—you had a lively evening and you got overtired. I'm not in a position to say, but I think that perhaps you have been doing too much all at once. I know it's lovely to see all your friends again, but you have so many . . .'

'I don't care if I never see any of them again. There's only one person I want to see, and he's miles away.'

'But I expect he'll come back some day?' suggested Suzannah comfortably, 'If you didn't do quite so much . . . by the time he does see you, you will be perfectly well and prettier than ever.'

She fetched some water and Julie gulped it down. 'Don't tell Mother.'

'No, but if Professor Bowers-Bentinck comes to see you and asks, I must tell him exactly how you are—or you can . . .'

'He'll just look at me and say nothing very much, but he won't be pleased. I never know what he's thinking.' She added pettishly, 'He's so old . . .'

'Is he?'

'I don't want to marry him after all—I thought he'd do instead of . . .' She broke off and glanced at Suzannah, who kept an uninterested expression on her face so that Julie went on, 'Oh, well, it doesn't matter. Someone else can have him and I wish her luck. Heaven knows, plenty of girls have tried.'

'I dare say he's wedded to his work . . .'

Julie, her fright forgotten, laughed. 'You are green, aren't you?'

'I'm afraid so. Would you like a hot drink?'

'No, but will you stay here until I go to sleep? That chair's quite comfortable.'

She took a long time to doze off, but at last Suzannah was able to creep back to her own cold bed and fall into a brief, troubled sleep before it was time to get up.

Julie was still asleep when she went down to breakfast. Mevrouw van Dijl had coffee in her room and her husband had left the house some time before; Suzannah sat down to her solitary meal.

She had just poured her coffee and was contemplating the basket of bread and rolls when the door opened and Anna came in. 'Professor Bowers-Bentinck,' she announced, and he walked past her and crossed the room unhurriedly to stand by her chair.

He stared down at her for a few moments and she stared back.

'Good morning, Suzannah. Why are you so pale?'

It would take too long to explain just then, so she said, 'Does anyone know you're here? Should I tell Mevrouw . . .?'

'Anna will do that.' He turned to say something to the maid and then sat down at the table. 'You won't mind if I share your breakfast? I'm on my way to a seminar in Amsterdam—it seemed a good idea to call in on my way.'

And, when she had nothing to say, 'And now tell me why you look so whey-faced.'

CHAPTER FIVE

'WHAT a beastly thing to say,' said Suzannah, finding her tongue at last. 'There's nothing wrong with me; we had rather a wakeful night.'

'Ah, yes, so I would imagine from the look of you . . .' He broke off as the butler came in with a tray: fresh coffee, eggs in a basket, toast, croissants and a variety of breads. He arranged these on the table before the professor, murmured *'smakelijk eten'* and went away.

The professor poured himself some coffee, examined the bread basket with interest, took an egg and helped himself to butter, perfectly at ease, and Suzannah, wishing to appear just as relaxed, asked, 'Do you often have breakfast here?'

He took a sip of coffee and added sugar, and although he spoke seriously she had the idea that he was amused.

'When Julie was ill, before I operated, I saw her frequently. This is a good time of day for a visit, before I start work . . .'

'Oh, yes—well. I thought you were in England.'

'So I was. I came over on the night ferry with the car; I've a couple of things to do while I'm here—I shall go back tonight.'

'Isn't that rather a rush?'

He shrugged. 'No, now let us apply ourselves to the matter in hand.' If he saw the quick colour come into her cheeks at his snub, he gave no sign. 'How is Julie?

I want your opinion, Suzannah—nothing professional.'

She said tartly, 'Well, I can't be that, can I? I'm not professional. She's been good-tempered for most of the time, although she doesn't like me being here, you know, and really it must be tiresome for her to have me trailing round all the time. When we're alone we get on very well . . .' She paused, remembering the nasty little slights she had had to put up with. 'Until last night she has slept for at least eight hours at a time and gone to bed at a reasonable hour, although she hated that. But last night was different; some friends came to see her and they didn't leave until late; she was a bit excited by the time that she was in bed. She woke crying, afraid that she was going to die and that you hadn't told her the truth when you said that she was cured. It took some time to settle her and she asked me to sit with her until she fell asleep.'

'And when was that?'

'About five o'clock.'

'And what did you tell her?'

'I told her at once that she wasn't going to die and that you wouldn't lie to her.'

'She believed you?'

'Oh, yes, after a time.'

'Has she talked to you about a young man she knew and who is abroad?'

'Yes. I think she loves him, only she believes that he doesn't love her. Sometimes she says that she will marry . . .'

She stopped and went a painful pink, and the professor said, 'Go on, Suzannah,! It is important that I know everything.'

'She sometimes says that she will marry you, only

then she changes her mind because you're too . . .'

'Old,' prompted the professor. 'As I am. I should point out to you that patients who have serious operations frequently believe themselves to be in love with the surgeon; it wears off the moment they realise that they are perfectly well again and resume a normal life.'

She stared at him thoughtfully. 'But isn't that awkward for you?'

'An occupational hazard, shall we say, and not all that frequent.' He took some toast and buttered it. 'Thank you for your help. And what about you?'

'Me? Oh, I'm fine.'

'You have your free time, your day off and your salary?'

'Yes, thank you.'

'I think that you have had to put up with Julie's occasional small rages; she can be shockingly rude.'

Suzannah said nothing and he went on, 'You feel that you can stay for another few weeks? Have you made any friends?'

She looked at him in astonishment. 'Good heavens, no—none of Julie's friends speaks to me.' And she added quickly, 'Well, why should they?'

'Why indeed?' He finished his coffee. 'Shall we go and see Julie now? Anna will have told her mother that I am here; I'll see her when I've examined Julie.'

'She's in bed.'

'Yes, I know that. I should like to see her before she has had time to realise I'm here.'

Julie was still asleep. She looked quite beautiful, her hair, grown again since her operation, framing her flushed face. The professor stood looking at her for a minute or two, and then picked up one arm flung across the counterpane. She woke then, staring at him, at first with bewilderment and then with delight. 'Guy—oh, I'm so glad to see you. Are you staying for a few days? Will you take me out one evening? Just us two?'

He leaned over the foot of the bed, smiling a little. 'I'm on my way to Amsterdam and it seemed a good idea to call in and see how you were. I'd like to take a look, if I may. It won't take long.'

She made a face. 'Don't you ever think of anything but your work? I feel fine.'

'Suzannah tells me that you have done exactly what I wished you to do; another week or two and you'll be out of my hands.'

He bent to examine her eye reflexes and then turn her head gently from side to side. 'Nothing hurts? You have a good appetite? Don't feel sick? Sleep well?'

Julie was sitting up in bed, her arms round her knees. 'I'm sure Suzannah told you everything. I can't move without her . . . I'm fine. Last night I had a bad dream, but it didn't last.'

The professor sat down on the side of the bed. 'You have nothing to worry about,' he told her, 'you have made a complete recovery but, just like anyone else, you need a little time to get over your operation. Do not do more than you have been doing; in a couple of weeks I'll let you off the hook for three months before I need see you again.'

'And Suzannah? Can she go?'

'In two or three weeks' time, yes.'

A remark which Suzannah heard with some trepidation.

He went away presently, and when Suzannah

encountered Mevrouw van Dijl later in the morning it was to hear that he had gone again. He could have said goodbye, thought Suzannah forlornly, listening to Mevrouw van Dijl's gentle voice. 'Such a dear little boy,' she was saying. 'I knew him a very long time ago, before I married, and when Julie was born he was a schoolboy and so good and kind to her. She was a difficult baby.'

She's a difficult grown woman too, thought Suzannah.

A few days later Julie's two brothers came. The elder, a rather solemn man in his late twenties, was married and had left his wife at home as she was expecting a baby. He was called Cornelius and, while he was obviously fond of his sister, he viewed her with a hint of disapproval; his brother on the other hand was very like Julie: good-looking and not averse to drawing attention to himself. They both worked in their father's business and were just back from America, and while Cornelius had little to say about their trip, Hebert was full of the places he had visited and the people he had met.

No one had thought of introducing Suzannah when they arrived. It was only when Julie said carelessly, 'I almost forgot, this is someone Guy wished on me until I'm perfectly well. Her name's Suzannah.'

Cornelius had said how do you do civilly enough, but Hebert had looked her over. 'Hello,' he said in fluent English. 'I wouldn't have your job for all the tea in China.' And he pulled a face and made her laugh. 'What do you think of Holland?'

'Well, I haven't seen enough of it to know,' she told him.

'Kept tied to Julie's heels? We must do something

about that.'

He pulled up a chair and, oblivious to his sister's black looks, began to tell Suzannah something of den Haag.

They were staying a few days, he told her, and when he discovered that she was free the next day he offered to show her round the city. Suzannah felt flattered and touched by his kindness, and, although she had intended to spend the day filling the gaps in her scanty wardrobe, she agreed at once. It would be pleasant to have someone to show her the high points of den Haag and was a chance not to be missed; perhaps she wouldn't be there for very much longer, and she might never come to Holland again.

The day was a success, it seemed to her, happily unaware of Hebert's careless amusement at her enthusiastic sightseeing. He mentioned it casually to Julie that evening, not meaning to be unkind but impatient of what he considered to have been a rather boring day.

'Well, it was your fault for asking her,' said Julie tartly.

'The girl doesn't get much fun; you must be the very devil to look after.' He sounded sulky and Julie laughed.

'You've done your good deed anyway, Hebert. We must hope that she doesn't expect any more outings with you.'

She need not have worried; Suzannah had enjoyed her day with Hebert but she had no expectation of it being repeated; for one thing, he would be gone again within a week, and she had only one day off in each week. He had been a pleasant companion, but she had the good sense to know that she was as unlike his usual companions as chalk from cheese. She went to bed content, although her contentment might not have been so undoubting if she had known that the professor had telephoned while she was out with Hebert and, since she hadn't been there to answer him, he had been put through to Julie who, feeling bored and bad-tempered, had embellished Suzannah's day out with her brother. The professor was no fool; all the same, even allowing for Julie's airy exaggerations, he found himself surprisingly put out. Suzannah was one of the world's Marthas, reliable and undemanding, surprisingly sharp-tongued when the occasion arose, but sensible and kind too. She had no business spending her day with Hebert, who was bent on amusing himself with not much thought of others. The professor was vexed to find that the idea of Hebert turning on his considerable charm in order to attract Suzannah was distasteful to him. He had put down the receiver with deliberation, his handsome features cast in a disapproving mould.

'Silly girl,' he remarked to the empty room. A remark both unfair and untrue and, coming from him, surprising.

He went back to England that evening and two days later flew off to Cairo for an urgent consultation and subsequent operation on an influential member of Middle East politics. He operated successfully and stayed in Cairo until the patient was out of danger, and if he thought about Suzannah at all during that time it was fleetingly.

Back in London, he satisfied himself that Julie's family doctor was happy with her progress and plunged into a backlog of work, so that it was almost three weeks before he went to Holland again.

Suzannah had found the three weeks irksome; Julie was, as far as she could judge, quite well again, but since she had promised the professor to try and curb Julie's activities she went on cajoling and persuading her to lead a moderately quiet life. A thankless task which earned her Julie's increasing impatience and peevishness.

Moreover, it was becoming increasingly difficult to get even an hour to herself during the day. Julie, rebellious about an afternoon nap, would rest only if Suzannah read to her, pointing out that she might just as well sit quietly with her as moon around on her own. That Suzannah had no intention of mooning once she was free to go out made no difference to her; if Suzannah stood firm and insisted on a couple of hours to herself while Julie rested, she would return to find the girl either in a state of hysterical rage which took the rest of the day to calm, or she would have phoned one of her friends and gone off in her car, coming back home hours later by which time Suzannah's nerves, not to mention her mother's, were worn to threads.

When the professor came she was determined to ask him if she might go back to England. She had very little idea of what she would do when she got there, but she had some money saved and, armed with a reference from Mevrouw van Dijl and one from the professor, she would surely find work.

She had managed to get her free days, but only after a good deal of arguing, and now, with another one due the next day, Hebert had come home for a day or so and, very much to her surprise, asked her if she would like to go to Panorama Mesdag, a vast painting on a circular canvas of Scheveningen. The building in which it was housed was in the centre of den Haag, and he suggested that they might go in the afternoon.

'I dare say you will want to shop in the morning; I'll meet you outside the Ridderzaal at two o'clock.'

She had intended to walk along Scheveningen's lengthy boulevard, have a snack lunch somewhere and go window shopping in the afternoon, giving the shops in den Haag a wide berth so that she wouldn't be too tempted to spend any money. The future began to loom, vague and uncertain, and money was the one thing she would need. Perhaps on her very last day off she would splash out.

She spent the morning wandering round the department stores, and after a cup of coffee went to the Mauritshuis and studied the paintings it housed before finding a small café and making another cup of coffee and a *kas broodje* last as long as possible. And presently it was time for her to find her way to the Ridderzaal. It was a chilly day and there was no one loitering there, so she walked up and down for ten minutes or so and was on the point of giving Hebert up when she saw him coming towards her. But not alone; he had a young woman with him, a pretty, fair girl, wrapped warmly and fashionably; not quite as young as Suzannah had first thought but exquisitely made-up, with fair hair falling in a silky cloud to her shoulders.

Hebert took Suzannah's arm and began walking rapidly away from the Ridderzaal. 'This is Monique, Suzannah, an old friend of mine.' He turned his head to laugh at the girl. 'She will join us for the afternoon . . .' He started an easy conversation which allowed Suzannah very little chance to talk, and from time to time he and Monique exchanged a low-voiced talk in Dutch so that by the time they reached Panorama Mesdag Suzannah was beginning to get the impression that she was *de trop*. Indeed, once they were inside she wished heartily that she hadn't come. But for the moment at least she forgot her awkwardness. They had entered through a series of rooms hung with Mesdag's paintings, and then at the end of a narrow passage they climbed a few steps and emerged to find a vast circular painting of Scheveningen in the late nineteenth century, so lifelike that she felt she must get over the guard rail and join the fishermen mending their nets by the North Sea. She went slowly, and it wasn't until she was half-way round that she realised that her companions were no longer to be seen. There weren't many people there, and those that were were engrossed in the vast painting, and they hardly noticed her hasty search round the circle. They weren't there; perhaps they had gone back to look at the paintings and would return presently. She told herself with her usual common sense that since she wasn't likely to see Panorama Mesdag again before she went back to England, she might as well complete her visit.

Fifteen minutes later she made her way out again, to pause at the entrance and look up and down the street. Dusk was still an hour or two away, but the afternoon was already becoming dim and it was difficult to see any distance. She waited for a few minutes and then turned her steps towards Noordeinde. She would have an early tea and then take a tram back to Scheveningen. She had gone only a few steps when she saw Hebert and Monique coming towards her.

'Suzannah, Monique remembered that she had to

collect something from the chemist and it seemed a good chance to go while you were looking at Panorama Mesdag; we did try to attract your attention inside, but you were so engrossed . . .' He laughed too loudly and went on quickly, 'Shall we have tea? There's a splendid place close by . . .'

Suzannah didn't believe a word; not only did he look guilty, Monique was looking decidedly uneasy. She agreed cheerfully to having tea, reminding herself that it was none of her business anyway, although she wondered why Hebert had asked her to be such an obvious third when he and Monique were, for the most part, unaware of her company.

The café to which he led them was hardly splendid. It was in a side street, clean as Dutch cafés were, however humble, and almost empty of customers. Hebert ordered tea, which came as glasses of hot water with a tea bag in each saucer, and a plate of little biscuits, and then, with a muttered excuse, carried on a low-voiced conversation with Monique.

Suzannah sipped her rather tepid tea and ate a biscuit, feeling lonely. When the other two paused for a moment she said, 'Well, thank you for showing me Panorama Mesdag and for my tea . . .' She intended to get up, but Hebert put out an urgent hand.

'Suzannah, you are a kind girl; will you do something for me—for us? I—we, that is—can only see each other secretly. Monique is married and I am engaged, but neither of us is happy. This is the only way we can meet. I ask you not to say anything to my parents—if you would let them think that we have spent the afternoon and evening together.' He added, 'They do not approve.'

'Well, I don't suppose they do,' said Suzannah. 'It seems rather hard on your fiancée and on Monique's husband. I won't tell. But don't think that I'll do this again for you, for I won't.'

She got to her feet, nodded briefly at them both and went into the street. It was almost dark by now and she wondered what she would do for the next hour or so. The shops were shutting and she was shy of going to a café on her own. It would have to be the cinema. She sat through an American film with Dutch subtitles, a combination which confused her, for a couple of hours, and then walked to the nearest tram stop.

The professor, driving through the city on his way to see Julie, stared at her small, hurrying figure, unable to stop because of the traffic lights. Her free day, he decided idly.

He was there sitting with Mevrouw van Dijl and Julie when Suzannah went into the drawing-room. He got to his feet, but before she could do more than greet them Hebert came in. The professor nodded coolly, having a poor opinion of him, but Hebert was effusive.

'Come to check on Julie, have you?' He wanted to know. 'She looks pretty fit to me.' He sat down close to Suzannah. 'I've been putting the car away. Suzannah and I had a delightful time in town—saw a few sights and had lunch and tea—introduced her to some of our famous cream cakes at Saur's and had a stroll round the shops afterwards.'

He laughed for no reason at all and glanced at Suzannah. 'We had a delightful time, didn't we, Suzannah?'

She didn't look at him and, since she was aware that the professor was watching her, she addressed her feet.

'Oh, very,' she agreed.

She was saved from saying more by Julie's rather petulant, 'Well, if you want to take a look at me, Guy, I suppose you'd better do it now. Suzannah, come with us—you can tidy up afterwards.'

Suzannah was only too glad to escape; perhaps by the time the professor had finished his examination Hebert would be gone. At least the professor wouldn't be there to hear her fibbing about her outing with Hebert.

He was in no hurry; he went over Julie with calm thoroughness, then sat down to talk to her while Suzannah fidgeted uneasily in the background. The moment she could, she would escape, she told herself, and was frustrated by the ringing of the telephone by the bed. When Julie went to answer it the professor said quietly, 'We'll wait outside,' and scooped Suzannah out of the room before she could think up a reason for staying.

He went to lean against the gallery rail overlooking the hall and turned to look at her. 'You had a delightful time with Hebert?' he wanted to know.

Suzannah turned a little way from him and became engrossed in the hall below. 'Yes.'

'It doesn't sound like him at all, looking into shop windows.' There was something in his voice which made her uneasy. 'I'm glad he gave you a good tea, though. Saur's is a delightful café—did you go upstairs?'

'Yes, yes, we did,' declared Suzannah, 'and the tea was splendid.'

'Although I don't care for that pink and gold china,' observed the professor.

The blandness of his voice made her glance quickly

at him. He returned the look with a smile as bland, and she was emboldened to say with foolish *sang froid,* 'I thought it rather pretty . . .'

He spoke very quietly in a voice to chill her to her bones. 'Suzannah, Saur's has no upstairs tea-room and certainly no pink and gold china; moreover, Hebert was not with you when I saw you walking down Lange Voorhout. Who did you spend the time with?' He watched her face. 'And don't waste time thinking up more lies—Oh, I dare say you were at Panorama Mesdag, it's an ideal place to meet and slip out again unobserved. But why, I wonder, did you and Hebert connive together?'

She very nearly choked. He had taken it for granted that she was meeting someone—a man—on the sly, and if that was what he thought of her he was even worse than she had always thought him to be, arrogant, narrow-minded, cold-blooded. 'It's none of your business,' she told him, but her voice, despite her best efforts, shook a little.

'Oh, but it is. I asked you to come here . . .' He stopped as two tears rolled down Suzannah's cheeks. She turned her back and wiped them away with a finger like a child. He said suddenly, 'I have it all wrong, haven't I? Hebert's up to his nasty tricks again and is using you. Oh, you don't need to fib any more, my dear, I shan't give him away, but neither will I permit him to do that to you.'

He turned her round to face him and lifted her chin to stare into her unhappy face. 'You don't like me, do you? But believe me, I wouldn't wish you any harm or any unhappiness.'

She made a small sound, a watery hiccup followed by

a sniff, and he offered her a very white handkerchief. 'When do you have your next free day?'

'Julie is going to visit an aunt next Thursday, Mevrouw van Dijl is going with her, and so it's convenient for them if I have my day off then.'

'Nine days' time . . .' He thought for a moment. 'I'll be over again on the Wednesday for a final visit until Julie's routine check-ups; I'll have the car and we will make a tour of some of the country.'

She regarded him with astonishment. 'But there's no need,' she told him urgently. 'Such a waste of your day, taking me out.'

'Oh, no, I shall enjoy seeing something of the Veluwe, it is a favourite time of year for me. And I dare say if we are very careful we shall manage not to disagree for an hour or so.'

He smiled then and she was quite taken aback to see his whole austere face alter; he looked kind and friendly, and at the same time comfortably detached. Perhaps, she thought confusedly, I shall like him after all. She nodded her bright head. 'I'd like to do that,' she told him, 'if you're sure it's not spoiling your leisure.'

He thought of the lunch with medical colleagues he would have to put off and the dinner he had intended to give to the charming daughter of an old family friend, and wondered why on earth he had so rashly committed himself to a day with this small, plain girl with the sharp tongue and the bright hair. He remembered the tears and smiled ruefully and, seeing her sharp look, said cheerfully. 'It is always a pleasure to show off one's adopted country.'

'I thought you were English.'

'I am, but my aunt married a Dutchman, as you

know, and I spent all my school holidays here, as well as taking a medical degree at Leiden.'

He spoke casually, and she thought that he might be getting bored; it was providential that Julie should join them then and presently all three of them went back to the drawing-room. After a little while the professor went away.

Suzannah contrived not to speak to Hebert during the evening; indeed, she rather felt that he was avoiding her while he talked loudly and at length about his work and the holiday he was planning to take. He gave so many details about it that it amounted to a timetable of his movements while he was away, so that Suzannah began to wonder if he and Monique had planned something together and he was trailing red herrings for his mother. That lady remarked during the evening that he was giving them such a detailed account of where he would be and what he would be doing that there would be no need for him to send postcards.

He had laughed heartily, and Julie had given him a quick look and giggled.

He stayed one more day and, since his father was at home, he spent a good part of it closeted in the study, discussing business. Beyond an occasional word, Suzannah had been able to keep away from him.

Julie had said nothing to her about her supposed outing with Hebert, and she decided that the girl knew more about it than she intended to say. She was growing impatient of Suzannah's company; although she rested reluctantly during the day and agreed to go to bed by midnight, there was always a tussle between the pair of them, with Julie lazing around her bedroom, lying for ages in the bath and then calling Suzannah back once she was in bed to fetch a book or a drink or whatever.

Suzannah didn't allow it to annoy her; the professor had said that his next visit would be the last until the three-monthly check-ups which meant that she would be leaving very soon now, and although she had been more than thankful for the job and she had been able to save most of her wages, she looked forward to being back in England. It would be lovely to see Horace again; the professor had told her that he was happy and had settled down very well, but the sooner she found a room so that he could be with her again, the better. The question of where she was to go on her return worried her; as soon as she knew when she was to return she would have to write to Mrs Coffin and ask if she and Horace might stay with her until she could find another job. She would have to collect Horace on the way, of course; she spent some time poring over timetables trying to fit in her journey to suit collecting him and going on to Mrs Coffin's on the same day.

True to his promise the professor arrived on the Wednesday, walking in as she sat at breakfast just as he had done previously. He wished her good morning civilly enough, ate his breakfast with only the modicum of conversation and asked her how Julie was.

He looked impatient, so she made her replies brief before they went upstairs to Julie's room. She was awake, drinking her morning tea and reading her letters, but she bounced up in bed as he went in and flung her arms round his neck.

'Very much better,' commented the professor. 'I wonder why.'

She waved a letter at him. 'He's coming home,' she

told him in an excited voice. 'Evert—you remember him?'

'Of course I do.' He added deliberately, 'You refused to let anyone tell him that you had a brain tumour . . .'

'Yes, but he says in his letter that he would never have gone away if he had known—how did he know?' She paused to puzzle over it.

'I wrote and told him,' said the professor placidly. 'You may have forgotten, but you never made me promise not to tell. He has been having weekly reports from me since I operated. I told him not to come back until you were quite cured. And you are. When does he get here?'

'Guy, oh, Guy—in two days' time. I thought I'd never see him again, and I didn't care what happened. I even thought for a little while that I'd marry you.'

The professor received this remark calmly. 'Well, now you won't have to, and as it happens I don't think I want to marry you; much as I find you very beautiful and charming! Now let us be serious for ten minutes and take a final and thorough look at you.'

Suzannah had been standing quietly a little apart, listening with the greatest interest, pleased that Julie's future was so rosy, and vaguely wistful and sad that something like that didn't happen to her. How easily her problems would be solved if a man were to appear, sweep her off her feet, marry her out of hand and never allow her to worry again for the rest of her life. She stood there daydreaming while the professor and Julie watched her. It wasn't until he had said, 'Suzannah,' for the third time that she came back to her senses.

'If you don't mind,' observed the professor, 'I would be glad if you would fetch Julie's pills—they need to be changed.'

She blushed and went to the bathroom to fetch them from the cupboard there. She thought he looked impatient again; she must vex him very much. He certainly wouldn't want to take her out as he had suggested. He must have been comforting her; people said all kinds of thing upon occasion and didn't mean them.

She offered the little bottles and Julie asked, 'When can Suzannah go? I don't need her now, you know. And when Evert comes . . .'

The professor didn't even look at Suzannah. 'He comes in two days' time—so, let me see, Suzannah can leave on the day after tomorrow. I will talk to your mother before I go.'

Julie flung her arms round his neck again. 'You really are a darling; you would make a lovely husband, only I can't think of a girl nice enough for you.' She looked at Suzannah. 'I don't suppose you've had much fun,' she commented. 'You'll be glad to get home and go out and about.'

Suzannah agreed smilingly. It was quite true, she reflected, half the world had no idea how the other half lived, and there was no point in enlightening Julie.

The professor patted Julie on the shoulder. 'Be a good girl,' he begged her. 'I'm going to see your mother now. You know where I am if you need help. Suzannah, come downstairs with me.'

In the hall he said, 'I'll be here at nine o'clock tomorrow; that will give us a long day out.'

'Oh, well, I thought . . . that is, I have to pack and look up trains and things.'

He swept an eye over her person. 'Packing will take

you half an hour, perhaps less; you haven't a very large wardrobe, have you? And you'll travel back with me—on the day ferry to Harwich—I booked you on to it.'

She goggled at him. 'But how did you know I would be leaving?'

'Well, of course I knew. Evert had told me that he would be coming and I was almost certain that I could discharge Julie, at least for the three months. You're no longer needed and I imagine you would wish to return to England. Unless you have some other plan?'

She shook her head. 'No. I mean to go to Mrs Coffin, if you wouldn't mind me picking up Horace on the way?'

'We'll talk about that tomorrow.' He studied her tweed skirt and jumper. 'Have you a winter coat? We might want to walk tomorrow and it has turned cold.'

She went a bright pink. 'Yes, thank you . . .'

'Good. I'll see you in the morning.' He nodded goodbye and crossed the hall to the drawing-room, leaving her to stand there, relief flooding through her because she wouldn't have to worry about the journey back. Even stronger than her relief was annoyance at his careless remarks about her clothes. 'It's all very well for him,' she muttered, going back upstairs, 'with his Bentley and his Savile Row suits and silk ties. Arranging things to suit himself.' An unfair remark, she admitted reluctantly; he had, after all, arranged for her return.

CHAPTER SIX

SUZANNAH stood in front of the dressing-table looking-glass and studied her reflection. It didn't please her. Her coat was a useful brown; it had been a good one some years ago, but it was faintly threadbare around the cuffs and down the front, and the brown dress beneath it did nothing to improve her appearance. She tucked a leaf-green scarf into the collar of the coat and, cold weather or not, decided not to wear the only hat she had: brown again and presumably prudently purchased with an eye to its usefulness rather than any pretentions to fashion. At least her gloves and handbag were passable. She wished suddenly that she hadn't accepted the professor's invitation, but it was too late to change things now and, thinking about it, he hadn't given her much chance to refuse. At this very moment he might be wishing that he wasn't to be saddled with her for a whole day.

His thoughts weren't quite as drastic as that; but as he drove through den Haag to pick her up he wondered why on earth he had asked her out. They had never had a real conversation, and for all he knew she would be tongue-tied, or, worse, chatty, and yet he found himself wishing to know more about her. And her eyes were beautiful. He thumped the door-knocker of the van Dijls' house and went in.

Suzannah came down the stairs, outwardly calm. She had been to see Julie, sitting up in bed enjoying her breakfast, and that young lady had thoughtlessly remarked that brown was all the wrong colour for Suzannah. 'You should wear green or that lovely greeny -blue tweed', she observed blithely, 'and of course you could wear black with that hair. Still, I don't suppose Guy will take you anywhere where he'll see anyone he knows.'

Suzannah had been quite unable to answer this; she had ducked out of the room and waited a moment before going down to the hall, rather pale with suppressed rage and humiliation. She crossed the hall to where the professor was standing and said good morning in a tight little voice, wanting very much to turn and run, only he said just the right thing. 'It's a cold, dark day and that hair of yours is like a ray of sunshine.' His smile was so warm that she found herself smiling in return, and suddenly the brown coat didn't matter at all.

In the car, sitting beside him in the greatest comfort, she was told to take the map from the pocket beside her. 'We shall go to Utrecht and then Appeldoorn and Zwolle, Kampen Sneek, across the Isselmeer, then across to Bergen and down the coast to Haarlem, across to Hiversum, then down the river Vecht—that's a beauty spot—and back here.'

'All in a day?'

'Holland is a small country, and we have eight or nine hours.' He smiled at her again, and she knew that the day was going to be fun, after all.

A few miles out of den Haag, the professor turned off the motorway, drove slowly through Gouda and took a secondary road through Oudewater, where he stopped the car to tell her about the witches' weighing scales there. She was surprised to find that he was both interesting and amusing, and when they reached Utrecht, although he didn't stop, he told her a good deal about the city as they drove through it.

Once out of the city he took another secondary road through the Veluwe, driving slowly so that she might enjoy the woods all around them, circumventing Appeldoorn and turning north to Vaasen where they stopped for coffee at a restaurant—'T Neotshuis. Its interior was spectacular and besides, close by was Kasteel Cannenburch, with its beginnings in the fourteenth century. The professor knew its history well, and over coffee he related it. 'Such a pity that it is closed, but the grounds are open if you would like to see them?'

'Yes, oh, yes, please,' said Suzannah, and skipped happily beside him out of the restaurant; she was feeling quite at ease despite her initial fears, and if her companion wasn't enjoying himself he was dissembling very successfully.

They drove on presently, to Zwolle and across the bridge to Kampen and then on to Sneek, where they stopped so that he might show her the harbour, crammed with yachts, and the Hoogeindster Waterpoort, an ancient water gate with two towers. She would have lingered there, for there was a great deal to see, but he whisked her back into the car and drove along narrow country roads winding beside the lakes stretching in all directions until they came to Beesterzwaag where they stopped for lunch. The hotel had a fine restaurant set in grounds which were still attractive, even at the tail end of the year. The food was delicious: smoked eel on toast, roast pheasant and red cabbage, and paper-thin pancakes with syrup. Over coffee, the professor said, 'We are about half-way; we shall drive over on the Afsluitdijk and cross over to the coast, the country there is pretty and the road is quiet until we reach Haarlem. We don't need to go into the town, we'll go south to Aalsmeer and turn off before we reach Hilversum and go down the river Vecht; the light will be going by then, but you will be able to see some of it. We can use the motorway from there, as it will be too dark to see any more.'

'We've been over almost all of Holland,' said Suzannah.

'It may seem like it to you; there are so many villages and small hidden roads still to discover.'

The weather stayed kind, although the afternoon was already darkening; the Afsluitdijk stretched unendingly, it seemed, but the Bentley made nonsense of its length. Then they were on the mainland again, taking a narrow road to the east coast. The professor had been right, it was pretty, with the sea never far off and small, isolated villages, but presently they reached the outskirts of Haarlem and turned inland on a main road now. But before they reached Hilversum he turned into a narrow, winding road running by a charming river, lined with trees and with splendid houses on either side of it; it was dusk now and they were lit, their high, wide windows uncurtained so that Suzannah longed to stop and walk up their wide driveways and peer inside. The professor knew several families living there and, seeing her interest, told her something of their history.

'It would be very nice to live here,' said Suzannah wistfully, 'but of course you live in England.'

He smiled a little and agreed. 'Shall we have a cup of tea? There's a café in Loenen.'

It was beginning to rain as they left the café, and there was a mean, cold wind blowing. The day was almost over and Suzannah was aware of regret; she had loved every minute of it and, surprisingly, she had liked being with the professor, although she still harboured the suspicion that he had given her a treat to make up for the small snubs and slights she had had. He was kind, she reflected, staring ahead of her into the dark, made darker by the car's headlights. They would be back in den Haag very soon now. She would spend the evening packing—well, she amended, part of the evening, for there was very little to pack. The professor had fallen silent and she began to brood over what she should do when she got back to England. But her thoughts were brought to an end by the professor's voice.

'I thought we might have dinner in Leidschendam, it's far too soon to go back.'

'Oh, yes—but I'm not dressed . . . I thought—that is, you might meet someone you know.'

'My dear girl, what are you talking about? I probably shall, but what has that got to do with us having dinner?'

'I think you might be ashamed of me,' she said in a cool little voice. 'I'm rather shabby, you know.'

His voice, very quiet, came to her through the dimness of the car.

'You must have a very low opinion of me, Suzannah.'

'Oh, no, I haven't, only . . .' She stopped just in time from telling him what Julie had said.

He finished for her, 'Ah, Julie in one of her bad moments planted the idea in your head.' He added coldly, 'And you believed her?'

'Not like that, I didn't.' She was anxious to explain, because she could hear the anger in his voice. 'I just didn't want to embarrass you. I don't think you'd mind a bit what I was wearing, but if you saw someone you knew they might—well, be surprised. I haven't explained very well, but I'm sorry you're angry, only it's true, I wouldn't want to embarrass you, truly I wouldn't.' She sniffed, a small, forlorn sound. 'It's been such a lovely day . . .'

'Indeed it has, and we are not going to spoil it now. We will dine at our ease and discuss what you are going to do next, and I promise you that you are quite adequately dressed: Julie's idea of shabby is wearing a dress for the second time, and hardly to be taken as a general rule.'

The restaurant, when they reached it, was a splendid one, and Suzannah cast the professor a reproachful look as her coat was taken from her, revealing the brown dress. A look which he ignored, and from the way the head waiter led them to a table with deferential respect she might just as well have been wearing a couture gown and diamonds.

The restaurant was already half full, and indeed the professor nodded to several people on the way to their table, but no one stared at her. Perhaps the dress wasn't so bad, after all.

The professor asked her what she would like to drink, ordered the sherry she asked for and a *jenever* for himself, and watched her while she studied the menu. The dress *was* terrible, he thought—someone should tell her to wear green or blue or grey—but he had to admit that her ordinary face, its colour heightened with excitement and, he suspected, misgiving, had a certain appeal; certainly her eyes were beautiful and the burnished copper of her hair was quite unusual. And she was a good companion . . . He smiled as she glanced up and asked her what she would like to eat.

'We had rather a large lunch,' she observed doubtfully, unaware that he had decided before they set out that he would at least give her a good lunch and dinner. Never one to do things by halves, and despite the fact that he had been regretting his invitation, he had kept faithfully to his plan.

He now found, rather to his surprise, that he was enjoying her company.

He said, 'That was hours ago. They do a very good salmon in lobster sauce—shall we have that? And perhaps a *mousseline* of chicken with caviare for starters? And, since we are celebrating Julie's complete recovery, I think we might have some champagne, don't you?'

Suzannah, relieved not to have to decide for herself, agreed and added artlessly, 'I had champagne once, on my mother's birthday . . .'

'And how long ago was that?' he asked gently, and led her on to talk about her childhood before asking casually, 'so what do you intend to do when you get back to England?'

It wasn't the first time he had asked her that. She reminded him that she would go to Mrs Coffin with Horace, and he said easily, 'Have you anywhere to stay in London? It occurs to me that it might be easier and far quicker for you if you were to leave Horace with Mrs Cobb for a few more days while you find a job.'

The champagne was having its effect; for the moment at least, life was benefiting from rose-coloured spectacles. 'Well,' said Suzannah cautiously, 'that would be much easier, wouldn't it? I could go straight to some employment agencies . . .'

'What do you have in mind?'

'I can't do shorthand and I don't know how to be a secretary, so I thought I'd try to get work as a receptionist at a doctor's or dentist's, but I'll take anything where I can have a room and keep Horace.'

'You have friends in London where you can stay when we get there?'

He reflected that he had helped her twice, and it looked as though he would be doing that for a third time. He didn't know whether to be relieved or not when she replied promptly, albeit untruthfully, 'Oh, yes. If Horace might stay until the next day with Mrs Cobb, just while I can get settled in.'

He frowned. 'Did you not say that you would stay with Mrs Coffin until you found work?'

'Yes, I did. But it seems a waste of time not to stay just a day or so in London first; I might get a job immediately.'

She spoke with conviction, made seemingly positive by her desire not to impose upon him a moment longer than she need. There must be lodgings somewhere in London where she could stay with Horace. Once there, even though it would be evening by then, she could say goodbye to the professor and find a place, if only for one night. Further than that she refused to think, shying away from a mental picture of her touring London with Horace in his basket, looking for work and a place in which to lay their heads. But, of course, if her search was fruitless she could get an evening train to Mrs Coffin's . . . She uttered a small sigh of relief and the professor wondered why, convinced that she was only telling him what she thought he would want to hear.

A patient man as well as a clever one, he began to talk about something quite different. Suzannah followed his lead so eagerly that he was more than ever sure that she was prevaricating. Time enough to find out when they got back to London. Hard on the thought came another; there was no earthly reason why he should concern himself with her future; he was seeing her safely back, she wasn't penniless and she had assured him that she would find work without any apparent difficulty. She was a sensible girl, well-educated and able to stand on her own two feet, and he could think of no reason for feeling concern for her future.

It wasn't mentioned again; the rest of dinner passed pleasantly, the talk of any number of subjects but never of her.

It was only a short drive back to the van Dijls' house, and once there he went in with her to spend half an hour in small talk with the van Dijls and Julie. When after ten minutes or so Suzannah excused herself on the grounds of packing her things, no one attempted to stop her from doing so. Beyond a brief nod of goodnight and the warning to be ready for him when he came to fetch her in the morning, the professor had nothing to say to her save to murmur a conventional rejoinder when she thanked him for her day. Perhaps he hadn't enjoyed himself as much as she had thought he had, she mused, getting ready for bed; it was difficult to know exactly what he thought about things at times. She went to sleep feeling vaguely worried, although she wasn't at all sure why.

He was exactly on time the next morning, and they

wasted very little time on goodbyes. Mijnheer van Dijl
was already at his office, but his wife thanked
Suzannah, kissed her and pressed a small packet into
her hands. 'You have been so good,' she murmured.
Julie trailed down in her dressing-gown to kiss the
professor and shake Suzannah's hand with a casual,
'Well, have fun wherever you are going. I won't stay; I
must get ready for Evert.'

'I hope you'll be very happy,' said Suzannah, and
got into the car, with the professor taking her case to
stow in the boot.

The journey was smooth and untroubled; the professor travelled without fuss, but with every detail dealt
with in advance. It was as they were nearing London in
a dark early evening that she said, 'If you would drop
me at Charing Cross station . . .'

He interrupted her. 'Certainly not, at this time of the
day. There is no question of you traipsing around
London on your own. It will be best if you come back
with me for the night; you can go to your friend's house
in the morning, and then come back and collect
Horace.'

'There is no need . . .' began Suzannah in what she
hoped was a firm voice.

'Don't argue.'

It was obvious to her that nothing she said would
alter his plan, so she said, 'Very well, Professor,' in
such a meek voice that he laughed.

They arrived at his house soon after that, and she was
ushered into its warmth and in no time at all found
herself sitting opposite to him at an oval dining-table in
an elegant dining-room, eating delicious food Mrs Cobb
had conjured up without any sign of fuss. And when

they had finished she was taken to the kitchen to see Horace. He looked sleek and content, but he was pleased to see her. He lived in great comfort, that was obvious, and she wondered how he would like the humbler home she hoped to find for them. The professor had gone to his study and she explained that in the morning she would go and see her friend, now so vivid in her imagination that she seemed real. 'And then I'll come back for Horace; I expect it will be after lunch . . .'

'That's all right, miss. The professor won't be here, but he said to expect you.'

Presently they said goodnight and Suzannah went out into the hall. She had been shown her room when they had arrived and she started up the stairs, uncertain whether to knock on the study door. It opened while she stood trying to make up her mind, and the professor stuck his head out.

'Going to bed? Sleep well. I shall be gone early and shan't be back until late in the evening. Collect Horace when you like; I've told Cobb to drive the pair of you and your case to your friend's house. Just let him know when you want to go.'

She said faintly, 'Oh, but there's no need,' and at his, 'Don't argue,' didn't finish but uttered her thanks for the journey. 'It was very kind of you,' she finished. 'Goodbye, Professor Bowers-Bentinck.'

He came out into the hall and stood looking up at her. 'We say goodbye rather frequently, don't we?' He added with a touch of impatience, 'Let me know if you need help. Have you sufficient money to keep you until you find a job?'

'Yes, thank you.' London was very much dearer

than her own small village; she pushed the worrying thought away and said cheerfully, 'And I can stay with my friend . . .'

He eyed her narrowly and was about to speak when the study door was pushed wide and a dachshund trotted out and sat down beside the professor. 'You haven't met Henry—come and say hello to him.'

She crossed the space between them and stooped to pat the little dog.

'Hello and goodbye, Henry,' she said, and rubbed a silky ear.

She stood up and offered a hand to the professor. 'Goodbye, Professor.'

He took her hand and bent and kissed her; she had been kissed before, though not often, casual kisses which had meant nothing, but this was different. The thought flashed through her mind that he was an older man, a man of the world, and must have had years of practice. It would be delightful to be kissed like that every day; she would have to be content with once in a lifetime. She said goodnight and goodbye in a brisk voice and went upstairs without a backward glance, reminding herself that there were a great many things about him that she didn't like; she couldn't call any of them to mind just at that moment, but she would certainly remember them later.

A pleasant girl brought her tea in the morning, told her that breakfast would be in half an hour and suggested she go to the breakfast-room on the left of the hall and warned her that it looked like snow. 'Just right,' she said cheerfully, 'with Christmas so near.'

Suzannah was met at the bottom of the stairs by Cobb with a cheerful good morning and the hope that she had slept well. 'I understand that you'll be going to your friend, miss. When you come back for Horace, I'm to drive you wherever you wish to go.'

She thanked him nicely and worried about it while she ate a splendid breakfast, went to say hello to Horace and presently got into her outdoor things and left the house.

It was now that she needed a kindly fate to step in and give her a hand, but in the meanwhile she would study the situations vacant columns of the daily press. She went into the first newsagents she came across once she had left the calm backwater where the professor lived, and, armed with several newspapers, walked on in the direction of Regent Street and in a small side street found a small, rather seedy café. With a cup of coffee before her, she opened the first of the papers and began searching.

Fate had decided to be kind; her eyes lighted upon an urgent demand for a young educated woman to help at a nursery school close to the Tottenham Court Road. The position was vacant due to illness and an address was added.

She left her coffee and crossed to the counter. 'Is Felix Road, just off the Tottenham Court Road, far from here?' she asked the man behind the coffee machine.

He scratched his head. 'Felix Road—that'll be near the 'ospital. Get on the underground to Goodge Street, it'll be close by. Yer can take a bus if yer want.' He thought a minute and told her the number. 'Might be 'andier.'

She thanked him and set off smartly, found a bus stop, caught a bus and presently got off again when the conductor warned her. She found Felix Road without much trouble: a narrow street in the warren of similar streets between the underground station and the hospital. The nursery school was half-way down it, a tall brick house needing a coat of paint, its neighbours on either side, apparently empty, even shabbier. But the windows were clean and curtained, and the neighbourhood was more or less traffic-free. She mounted the steps to the front door and rang the bell.

She could hear children's voices from behind the door, and someone singing nursery rhymes, and when the door opened the woman standing there was reassuringly middle-aged and motherly.

She eyed Suzannah. 'Yes?' she asked.

'There is an advertisement,' began Suzannah, and before she could say more she was invited in.

'Perhaps it is already filled?'

The older woman held out a hand. 'Mrs Willis. I own this place.'

'Suzannah Lightfoot.'

They shook hands and the woman said, 'No, there have been several girls after it, but it's too much like hard work for most, and they don't like the idea of living here.'

She opened a door in the hall. 'Come in and I'll explain.'

They sat facing each other across a small table in the rather bare room. 'I've lost two of my helpers in the last week: one is ill, the other got married. There are thirty children here, toddlers; most of the mothers work at the hospital and the toy museum down the road. They come at eight o'clock in the morning and most of the kids are called for by six o'clock each evening. It's hard work and the pay's not much—it's not state-run——'

She mentioned a sum which Suzannah thought she could manage on if she were careful. 'There's a bedsit in the basement, and you'd have to live in. Sundays off and most Saturday afternoons. It's quiet here, not a bad area, although it's a bit run-down. I live at the top of the house, but I must warn you that once I'm there of an evening, I don't want to be disturbed.' She stared across the table at Suzannah. 'Have you references?'

Suzannah handed them over. A letter from Lady Manbrook, another one from Mijnheer van Dijl and one from the vicar at home. Mrs Willis read them carefully. 'Done any teaching?'

'No. I have four A-levels and have been offered a place at a university. I couldn't take it up because the aunt I lived with became ill.'

'I usually check references, but I'm pretty desperate for help. How do you feel about coming here? A month's trial?'

'I should like to work here. I have a cat; may he live here in the bed-sitting-room?'

'Why not, as long as he's not a nuisance? You'd better come and see the place.'

She led the way out of the front door and down the area steps to another door beneath them, took a key from her pocket and unlocked it. The room was rather dark and cold, but it was clean, with a small gas stove in one corner and a door leading to a toilet and shower-room. The furniture was sparse and cheap, but the curtains were cheerful and there was a small gas fire in front of the old-fashioned grate.

'It's rent-free,' said Mrs Willis. 'Goes with the job. You can bring any bits and pieces of your own.'

'I haven't any. I'd like the job, Mrs Willis, and I

could move in today if you would like me to. If I could have an hour or two to settle in and get some milk and bread and food, I could start first thing in the morning.'

'Want the job that bad?'

'Yes, I do. And I'll work hard.'

Mrs Willis smiled. 'Let's hope you can kept it up. We don't have holidays here like the schools. I close on Christmas Day and Boxing Day and at Easter for a couple of days, but the women around here work most of their days and there's nowhere to take the kids. Any plans for Christmas?'

'None, Mrs Willis.'

'Good. I'm going over to my sister's at Northolt as soon as the last child's gone on Christmas Eve, and I'll be back late on Boxing Day. Mind being here alone?'

'No, I don't think so.'

'The houses on either side, they're used as warehouses for small firms, but there are folk living across the street and further down the road.'

She handed Suzannah a key. 'Let yourself out and come back when you're ready. You'd better see round the place then. I can't spare the time now.'

Well, she had a job and somewhere to live, thought Suzannah on her way back to the professor's house. Not ideal, but better than nothing, and since she was to be paid weekly she could afford to lay out some of the money she had on a store of groceries and one or two small comforts.

She had some difficulty in persuading Cobb to allow her to leave in the taxi she had prudently hired. 'I don't know what the professor will say,' he said worriedly. 'I was to see you safe and sound at your friend's house . . .'

'Well, he didn't know—and nor did I—that my

friend would get a taxi to bring me back here to collect
Horace and my things. It's outside now, waiting. Could
you explain that to the professor? And tell him that I've
got a good job with a nice little flatlet.' She shook his
hand. 'Thank you and Mrs Cobb, and please thank the
professor for me; I'll write to him.'

So Cobb had let her go, looking doubtful still and
presently she was back in the basement room, making a
list of the things she would need, with Horace, glad to
see her but not best pleased with his surroundings, sitting suggestively before the unlit fire.

She put fifty pence in the slot and lit it before she
hurried out to the few shops she had seen at the end of
the street. At that hour of the afternoon there weren't
many shoppers; she bought what she needed, prudently
stocking up on tins of soup, then she ordered milk and
collected bread and food for Horace and hurried back
again. With the curtains drawn and the light on, the
room didn't look too bad. She fed Horace and made a
cup of tea for herself, filled the hot-water bottle she had
bought and put it in the divan bed in one corner and
went back up the steps to the front door.

It was open now and there were women coming and
going, collecting children after their day's work. Mrs
Willis saw the last of them away, said goodnight to a
dispirited-looking girl who followed them out and who,
it transpired, was another teacher, and led Suzannah
round the house. The rooms were given over to the
children: four quite large rooms on the ground floor,
although with two helpers short she and the girl had
been managing between them in two of the rooms.
'We'll split the children up tomorrow, that will mean
ten or twelve each. They play and learn a bit until noon,

then they have their dinners and you and Melanie take it in turns to keep an eye on them all while they rest for an hour. So every other day you'll get a bit of free time for shopping. We close at five o'clock, though sometimes I'll keep a child until six if the mother can't get here before then.'

All the while she had been talking she had been marching round the house, pointing out where everything was kept. It was all very clean and there were small hand-basins in the cloakroom and a long, low table with small chairs for the children's meals.

'You and Melanie eat with the children, but you get your own tea and take it in turns to have it. We open at eight o'clock, so have your breakfast first.'

They were back at the front door again. 'I said before that it's hard work but I treat you fairly, and if you can't stick it, just say so.'

It was nice to have Horace to talk to; Suzannah aired her plans and doubts to him while she got her supper ready. The contrast between their new home and her comfortable bedroom at the van Dijls' was cruel, but that was something she could remedy, given time and money; in the meantime, she assured him, they would be cosy enough. He was a docile cat and had quickly discovered that, although he might go into the concreted area, that was his limit. She arranged an old woolly scarf before the fire and he curled up without fuss.

At least the water was hot in the shower and the room had warmed up nicely; she ate her supper, made a list of shopping and went to bed. To her surprise her last thoughts were of the professor. Rather sad, although she didn't know why.

He was thinking of her too, but without sadness.

Cobb, when questioned, had been unable to give any accurate information as to where Suzannah had gone, and the professor was fair-minded enough not to blame him for letting her leave without giving an address, but he was annoyed that she should go in such a fashion. Almost as though she didn't want him to know just where she had gone; she should have remained at his house until he had made sure that this good job really was good. He frowned; the wretched girl was intruding too deeply into his busy life and it was nonsensical of him to concern himself with her; she had shown clearly enough that she was quite capable of looking after herself. But a nagging doubt remained; he felt compelled to telephone first his aunts and then Mrs Coffin, asking them to let him know if Suzannah should get in touch with them.

Suzannah was up early, breakfasted and tidied her room and had seen to Horace and was ready in the hall when the first of the toddlers arrived. And after that the day became too busy to think. The children for the most part were good, but they needed amusing, and the older ones had to be given simple lessons. Midday dinner was chaotic but thankfully, when it was over, the children were ready to rest for an hour or so. Suzannah had agreed to mind them while Melanie had her free hour, and Melanie, glad to have someone to help her, agreed to Suzannah slipping down to her room to see Horace before she went. She was a melancholy girl but, like Suzannah, needed to earn her own living, and she was good with the children. She lived with a widowed mother at the other end of the street and had a boy-friend who wanted to marry her. 'Only of course there's Mother,' said Melanie. 'She doesn't like him overmuch and won't have him to live at home, so we have to wait until we can find rooms or a small flat.'

Suzannah listened with sympathy, begged her not to hurry back and settled down to watch over the toddlers, arranged in neat rows to sleep. The day seemed endless, but the next day was easier; it was her turn to be free while the children rested and she went shopping with an eye to Christmas, now so close. She found the public library too and chose two books. When she returned she spent a short time with Horace and went back to sing nursery rhymes with the ten children she was looking after.

She saw very little of Mrs Willis, but on the second day, as they passed each other in the hall, she paused long enough to ask if Suzannah was managing and was she warm enough in her room?

Suzannah said cheerfully that she was perfectly happy and everything was fine. All the same, she cried herself to sleep that night. Even with Horace for company, she was lonely.

On Christmas Eve the children had a party so that they were fetched a little later than usual, and when they had all gone the three teachers cleared away the cardboard plates and mugs, tidied the place, wished each other a happy Christmas and went their separate ways. By early evening the house was quiet, for Mrs Willis had gone and so had Melanie, and Suzannah was very conscious of the silence, even with the radio on. She had bought a chicken already cooked, sausage rolls and a few mince pies and a few sprigs of holly. She would go to church in the morning, she decided, and on Boxing Day go for a walk in one of the parks.

She ate a mince pie, gave Horace an extra snack of

sardines, drew the rather down-at-heel armchair close to the gas fire and settled down to read.

She wasn't a girl to mope; all the same she was quite glad to think that the place would be open the next morning as she got ready for bed on Boxing Night. She had gone to church on Christmas morning and come back to share the chicken with Horace and listen to the radio, and on Boxing Day she had gone for a really long walk, finding her way to Green Park and then into St James's Park and walking all the way back again. She had had a good think as she walked, and she knew what she was going to do: stay with Mrs Willis for six months and then apply to one of the London hospitals to train as a nurse. She would have liked to have done that sooner, but there was the problem of Horace; she would need to save enough money to rent a room so that she could live out while she trained, and if she was careful and saved every penny she could spare and added it to the money she already had, she would be able to manage on a student nurse's pay. She had walked the long way back, doing mental arithmetic and pondering ways and means; the results weren't always very clear, for the sums kept coming out differently because she found that her thoughts were sidetracked far too often by thoughts of Professor Bowers-Bentinck.

'And I can't think why,' she observed crossly to Horace, 'for he was a ship passing in the night, as they say.'

She was more than busy when the children arrived in the morning; most of them were tired, queasy from too many sweets and pettish and whiney in consequence. She spent a good deal of her day mopping up after puking toddlers, and the rest-hour was a nightmare of grizzling moppets. They were feeling more themselves on the next day, and since it was her turn to have an hour off in the afternoon she was able to go to the shops and stock up once more, and after that everyone fell easily enough into the usual routine. It was broken again at the New Year, but only for a day, and Suzannah, now quite at home in her job, hardly noticed the small upsets caused by upset tummies and a rash of head colds.

She had been there rather more than a month when Mrs Willis decided that the children, well wrapped up against the cold, should be taken for a short walk twice a week. Suzannah and Melanie welcomed the idea; it would fill in the later part of the morning before dinner, and it would be nice to have a breath of air. A school-leaver glad of the pocket money agreed to give a hand, and the first expedition went well. The children were, on the whole, good, and the weather, though cold, was bright and it made a nice change for everyone.

The dry, cold weather held and the morning walks became part of the week's regime, down side streets, across the Tottenham Court Road and ten minutes running around in the grassy square on the other side and then back again.

It was when the procession of small children was wending its toddling way back, with Melanie in front, the teenager in the middle and Suzannah bringing up the rear, carrying a reluctant walker, that Professor Bowers-Bentinck, waiting at the traffic lights for the slow-moving procession to trot across the road, saw Suzannah, one toddler clinging round her neck, another held by the hand, making her careful way behind the string of small people.

Shaken from his usual calm, he uttered a startling sound between a groan and a great sigh, and only when the driver behind him hooted urgently did he see that the lights were green again and the wavering crocodile was disappearing down a street on the opposite side. He had perforce to drive on, but presently he found a side turning, reversed the car and drove back the way he had come, to stop by a parking meter, get out and make his way to the row of shops across the pavement.

He tried several shops before he found somebody who could answer his questions. Oh, yes, said the beady-eyed old lady behind the counter in the general stores, there was a nursery school not too far away. 'Want to send the little 'uns there?' she wanted to know. 'Well, you could do worse than Mrs Willis. Takes the kids when the mums go to work, and one or two besides.' She paused infuriatingly to think and scratch her permed head with a pencil. 'Felix Road, that's where she is. Near the hospital.'

The professor thanked her with a suave charm which left her smiling, and went back to the Bentley. He had no difficulty in finding Felix Road, and he drew up outside the house, spent a few minutes telephoning to his registrar and sat, a prey to a number of thoughts. But when he saw the door open and Suzannah go down the steps to her basement, he got out and followed her without hurry.

It was her turn to have an hour off. She was feeding Horace when the door-knocker was thumped. She opened it and the professor walked in.

CHAPTER SEVEN

THE professor walked in without hesitation, so that Suzannah retreated before him until she came up against the table and couldn't go back any further. It took her a moment or so to find her voice, surprise and a sensation she had no time to guess at had taken her breath, so that her, 'Hello,' was uttered in a strangled squeak.

Rather disconcertingly, he said nothing, merely stood there, looming over her, his ice-blue eyes cold. Presently he took his gaze from her face and studied his surroundings. When he spoke, his voice was quiet and gentle.

'You were going to write,' he said mildly.

She could see that he was coldly angry, despite his tolerant tones.

'Yes, well, I did mean to, and then I thought it was a bit silly . . .' He raised his eyebrows and she hurried on, 'I mean, you're busy, going here and there and everywhere, and important too, I dare say, and you must have a great many friends. We weren't likely to see each other again—there seemed no point . . .' Her voice petered out under his stare.

He said harshly, 'I see. But was it necessary to lie to me, Suzannah?'

She went red. 'I'm sorry about that, but I didn't want to be a nuisance; you have done such a lot for me—I can't think why.'

'Nor can I.' A reply which she found disconcerting.

She said politely, 'Will you sit down. I have to go back to the children in half an hour or so; it's my free hour—we take it in turns.'

He sat down on the wooden chair at the table and it creaked alarmingly. He asked casually, 'You live here? The other teachers too?'

'Mrs Willis, the one who owns the school, lives on the top floor in a proper flat. Melanie, the other helper, lives with her mother at the end of the street.'

'And do you intend to make this your life's work?'

'Oh, no. I thought I'd stay here for six months, then I can train as a nurse.'

'Why not sooner than that?'

'Well, I'll need to have a room and live out because of Horace.'

She was sitting on the edge of the divan, her hands in her lap.

'I've had time to think about it. I don't want to teach; I like children, but I don't think I'd make a good teacher.'

'So you have your future settled.'

'Yes. How did you know I was here?'

'You crossed the road with a string of infants a short while ago; I was waiting at the traffic lights and my curiosity got the better of me.' He gave her a hooded glance. 'Are you lonely, Suzannah? Where did you spend Christmas?'

'No. I'm too busy to be lonely.' She said it too quickly, without looking at him. 'I spent Christmas here.'

'Alone?'

'I had Horace.' She spoke defiantly, uneasy at his questions. 'I really am very happy.'

He got to his feet, dwarfing everything around him. 'I am delighted to hear it.' He smiled thinly. 'Do you want me to go?'

'Yes. I have a great deal to do . . .'

'You said that once before,' he reminded her. 'And once before I came to see if I could help you, but it seems that I am once more mistaken.'

He went to the door and with his hand on the door knob turned to ask, 'There was no friend, was there, Suzannah?'

'No.'

He nodded his head and opened the door, and went up the steps, got into his car and drove away.

She stood listening to the Bentley's quiet departure and made no move to sit down. 'I don't suppose I shall ever see him again,' she told Horace. 'I said all the wrong things, didn't I? I didn't even thank him for coming to see me, and there was no need for him to have done that. I thought I didn't like him, but I think I do, even when he's angry and goes all icy and quiet!' There seemed no reason why she should burst into tears, but she did, so that when she went back presently and Melanie commented upon her puffy eyes and red nose, she had to pretend that she had a cold.

She found the days passing very slowly. They were not monotonous, for thirty small children each doing his or her own thing hardly made for monotony, but they needed to be played with, taught their letters, how to count, how to feed themselves, and they needed to be cuddled and amused and kept clean. Suzannah was tired by the end of the day, and yet she went to her room reluctantly when the last of the children had been fetched home. She had told the professor stoutly that she

wasn't lonely, but that hadn't been true; despite
Horace's cosy presence, she longed for someone to talk
to. Preferably the professor; she admitted that, to her
own astonishment. They might dislike each other, but
even while he was poking his nose into her affairs he was
reassuringly large and dependable; moreover, when he
chose, he was a delightful companion. 'Although I don't
like. him,' she told Horace, too often and too loudly.

It was a couple of weeks later, well into the middle of
a snowy February, that fate took a hand once again.
The children hadn't gone out that morning—the
weather was too bad. They sat at their little tables,
painting and modelling with clay, evenly divided
between Suzannah and Melanie while Mrs Willis had
gone to supervise their dinners being prepared in the
kitchen at the back of the house.

Suzannah, scraping modelling clay off an over-
enthusiastic moppet, twitched her small nose and then
frowned. There was a faint smell of burning and not
from the kitchen, for it was acrid, like scorching cloth.

Melanie was in the adjoining room with the door
half-open. Suzannah opened it wide and called her, and
then, as the smell was suddenly stronger and she could
hear a faint crackling, she shouted urgently.

Melanie came across the room, frowning. 'That's no
way to talk in front of the kids,' she began. 'Someone's
burning the dinner . . .'

'I'm going to see what it is; look after my lot,' said
Suzannah, and didn't wait for an answer. She shut the
door after her and went into the hall. The kitchen was
beyond the staircase and she could hear voices from it;
the crackling was coming from somewhere upstairs, and
as she began to run up them a puff of smoke eddied

from under a door on the landing.

It was the door leading to Mrs Willis's flat, and it was locked. She tore down the stairs again, breathless with fright, flung open the kitchen door and found the room empty. Mrs Willis and the cook were in the small room beyond where the bowls and the spoons were kept.

'There's a fire in your flat, Mrs Willis,' said Suzannah, and without waiting for an answer she raced back again to where Melanie was rounding up the children for their dinners.

'Don't ask questions—there's a fire upstairs, get the children's coats and get them out—quick!'

Melanie was a nice girl, but not quick on the uptake. 'Fire?' she asked. 'I thought it was the kitchen burning something . . .'

'Oh, be quick, do!' cried Suzannah, quite out of patience as well as being scared to death. She went to the small cloakroom off the hall and hauled out coats and hats and scarves and began putting them on the children whether they belonged or not. She was aware that Melanie had rushed up to her, clutching her arm, shouting that there was a fire and they must get out of the house, but she shook her off, still bundling the children into coats. 'Of course there's a fire!' she shouted. 'The children will catch their deaths without coats; for heaven's sake wrap them up and get them out.'

Mrs Willis and the cook were there now, marshalling the children into the hall and out through the door and down the steps.

'I've phoned the fire brigade,' shouted Mrs Willis. 'Get the children counted.' A blast of unpleasantly hot air billowed down the stairs and she coughed. The last of the children were being hustled out when one small boy turned and ran back into the second of the playrooms. The smoke was thick now and a small tongue of flame whipped round the top of the stairs. Suzannah snatched up a woolly scarf, wound it round her face and plunged into the smoke. The child was at the back of the room, still comparatively free from smoke, searching frantically through the box of toys in one corner. Suzannah saw who it was then: Billy Reeves, small and undernourished and inseparable from the grubby teddy bear he dragged with him each day. Common sense told her that it was madness to delay there, but it might be quicker to find the bear and hurry Billy away from danger than try and prise him loose from something he was determined to do. She had learned a lot since she had joined the staff at the nursery school.

Spurred on by the child's frustrated screams and sheer terror lest they wouldn't be able to get out of the house, she hurled toys in all directions, found the bear, snatched up a suddenly happy Billy and rushed out into the hall. The stairs were well alight now, although the flames were not yet half-way down, but the smoke was worse. She clapped a hand over Billy's mouth and nose and ran to the door just as the wooden ceiling above their heads began to fall in. A smouldering plank fell across them, and she pushed it away with a free hand, not noticing the pain as it scorched her. She almost fell through the open door and pushed Billy into Mrs Willis's waiting arms.

'Horace,' she shouted to no one in particular, and galloped down the area steps to scoop him into his basket and rush back again. There was quite a crowd by now, and the fire engine's reassuring siren very close, and hard on its heels a police car and an ambulance.

None of the children was hurt, but they were terrified and cold; they were stowed into the ambulance and taken the short distance to the hospital and a second ambulance took the rest and Melanie. Mrs Willis refused to go, and Suzannah, shivering with cold and well aware of her throbbing hand, stayed with her. Mrs Willis, usually so efficient, looked as though she would faint at any moment. She clutched Suzannah as the fire took hold. 'My flat,' she muttered, 'and all the work I've put into the place . . .'

Suzannah put an arm round her. 'The children are safe; you'll get insurance and be able to buy another house. And there must be an empty hall or rooms where you can carry on—the children will need you.'

Mrs Willis blew her nose and wiped her eyes. 'You're right, it isn't the end of the world. I've plenty of friends, too.'

She saw that Suzannah was shivering and noticed her hand. 'You're hurt, you must go to hospital and have that burn dressed. You were very brave to go after Billy. I should have gone . . .'

'I was the nearest,' said Suzannah, and broke off as a police officer tapped her on the shoulder. 'We'll run you to the hospital, miss. That hand needs seeing to. There's nothing more to do here. And you too, ma'am. You're the owner? No need for you to catch your death of cold; we'll drop you off if you've friends who'll put you up until things are sorted out.'

'At the end of this street.' Mrs Willis got into the car beside Suzannah. 'And what about you, Suzannah? Have you somewhere to go when you've had your hand seen to?'

Suzannah had Horace's basket on her lap; his head was pressed up to the wires at its end and she was stroking him with a finger. She said cheerfully, 'Oh, yes, I'll be all right, Mrs Willis.' The poor woman had enough to worry her.

The accident room was busy. Suzannah was sat down in a chair and told that someone would see her in a few minutes. The minutes ticked away while two road accidents were dealt with one after the other, which gave her more than enough time to wonder what she would do. She had no money and no clothes, only Horace, quiet in his basket beside her. She supposed that someone would tell her where she could get a bed for the night; the Salvation Army or perhaps the police would help. A cell, perhaps . . . She giggled tiredly and closed her eyes.

And that was how the professor found her; he had been called down to give his opinion of a severe head injury, and on his way back to the consultant's room he saw her. She was a deplorable sight and smelled horribly of smoke. Her hair was full of bits and pieces and specks of soot, and there was a smear down the front of her skirt and the sleeve of her sweater was badly scorched. She had laid her burned hand across her chest to ease the pain, while the other hand clutched Horace's basket.

The professor said something forcibly under his breath, and the house doctor with him said quickly, 'I expect she's from the nursery school. There's been a fire there—the children came here to be checked, none of them hurt, luckily.'

'When was this?'

'Oh, an hour or so ago, sir.'

The professor swore quietly and the young surgeon looked at him in surprise. Professor Bowers-Bentinck never swore and seldom raised his voice, certainly never before a patient; he had the reputation of being a rather cold man, brilliant at his work and certainly very sure of himself.

'I know this young lady,' said the professor. 'I want her taken up to theatre—they'll be busy in the two main theatres, so put her in the surgery at the end, will you? Get a porter and do it now, if you please.'

She woke up when the porter brought a chair and, still clutching Horace's basket, only half awake, she was transported to the fourth floor where the theatre block was.

The surgery was a small room used for taking out stitches and minor cuts and dressings, and the young surgeon hovered round her, not quite sure what to do. He had suggested leaving the cat basket outside, but Suzannah had clung to it and even tried to get up and go. And, since the professor had left her in his care, the young man was in two minds as to what to do.

Suzannah sat watching him; any minute now he might snatch Horace from her and he was all she had left in the world. Two large tears trickled down her dirty cheeks.

The professor, coming quietly into the room with everything needed to deal with her hand, dumped the lot on his houseman, whipped out a very white handkerchief and wiped her face.

'Oh, it's you,' wailed Suzannah, and gave a really tremendous sniff.

He took Horace's basket from her and put it on the floor.

'Indeed it is I. No, don't worry about Horace, he'll not be taken away. I will see to that hand before I take you to Mrs Cobb for the night.'

Suzannah sniffed, blew her nose, wiped her eyes once more and said, 'No,' and because that sounded rather rude, 'Thank you very much, but I'll be all right.'

The professor didn't bother to answer. He beckoned his houseman nearer and began to clean her hand and dress it. He was gentle, but it hurt all the same. When she spoke it was because she felt that someone should say something. 'I thought you were a brain surgeon.'

'Oh, I am, but one does acquire the rudiments of first aid as well.'

A remark which drew forth an outraged snort from the house doctor.

The professor finished the job to his satisfaction and said, in the kind of voice which brooked no arguing, 'You will wait here, Suzannah, with Horace. I shall return in about ten minutes.'

Whatever he had done to her hand had soothed it; the throbbing pain had eased and her one wish was to be allowed to sleep. She was scarcely aware of his going, and dozed off while the house doctor, left to mount guard, tidied away the considerable mess the professor had made.

She awoke when the professor came back, this time with a porter and a chair, and although she attempted to remonstrate with him he took no notice, but disappeared again. She was wheeled through endless corridors and into lifts and at last was trundled through a side door of the hospital.

The Bentley was there; the professor shovelled her carefully into the seat beside his, put Horace in the back of the car, thanked his assistants gravely and drove away.

Suzannah, more or less free from pain and her lungs clear of smoke, had revived. She said worriedly, 'I smell awful,' and then, 'Where are you taking me?'

'Back to my house. Mrs Cobb will take care of you. Tomorrow you can decide what you want to do. A little while ago you told me that you would be quite all right, but at the moment you are in no fit state to go anywhere but to bed.'

The word bed conjured up the blissful thought of sleep. 'And you don't mind having Horace, too?'

'I have no doubt that Mrs Cobb will be delighted.'

He sounded impatient and she said nothing more; once she had had a good sleep, she told herself, she would think of what to do.

At his house he handed her over to Mrs Cobb, who tutted softly, gave Horace into Cobb's care and led Suzannah upstairs. 'A nice warm bath,' she said comfortably, 'and something tasty for your tea and then bed.'

'Tea?' asked Suzannah, 'I don't know what the time is . . .'

'You poor child, you're worn to a thread. The professor said you had been in a fire and got burnt, and very nasty that must have been.'

She began to remove Suzannah's clothes. 'And I'll do what I can with this skirt and jumper of yours, but they are really beyond my skill. Of course, you've no clothes . . . Did they save anything from the fire?'

Suzannah was in the bath, her injured hand resting on its side. 'I don't know.'

She sounded near to tears, and Mrs Cobb said

quickly, 'Well, no matter, but I'll wash that hair of yours.'

And presently, tucked up in bed, a light meal and a pot of tea disposed of under Mrs Cobb's motherly eye, she curled up and slept. The bed was soft and warm, and she had no doubt that the room she was in was delightful, only she was too tired to bother to look.

The professor, coming home an hour or so later, was led upstairs by his housekeeper. 'Just so's you can see the young lady's all right,' said Mrs Cobb. 'Very tired, she was and, begging your pardon, sir, filthy dirty.'

They stood together looking at Suzannah, deeply asleep—indeed, snoring very delicately.

'I hear at the hospital that she went back into the fire to fetch a small boy who had escaped to find his teddy bear.'

'Well, fancy that!' declared Mrs Cobb. 'Poor lamb, it's a wonder that her wits aren't turned.'

The professor said gravely, 'Fortunately I believe Miss Lightfoot to be a young lady who will always keep her wits about her.'

They went back downstairs and he passed her and paused on his way to the study. 'I'm dining out, Mrs Cobb. Don't wait up—tell Cobb to lock up if I'm not back by eleven o'clock.'

It was a long-standing engagement he couldn't put off, but he excused himself as soon as he reasonably could, getting home just before Cobb began his evening round.

'I'll be in the study, Cobb. Ask Mrs Cobb to look in on Miss Lightfoot before she goes to bed, will you?' He opened his study door. 'I'll take a look as I go to bed.'

He said goodnight and sat down behind his desk.

There were letters to answer and reading to be done. It was almost one o'clock when he got to his feet at last and went upstairs.

Suzannah, refreshed by her sleep, sat up in bed and looked around her. There was a rose-shaded lamp by the bed and the room looked charming in its soft glow. The furniture was maple, and the curtains and bedspread were rose-patterned in some heavy silk fabric. She examined it all slowly, aware at the same time that her hand was increasingly painful, and not only that, she was hungry. The dainty little carriage clock on the tallboy said half-past twelve. Everyone would be in bed by now. She lay back again and closed her eyes, but now sleep eluded her, and if she shut her eyes she could see the flames creeping further down the stairs and remember how terrified she had been while she and Billy searched for his teddy bear; the picture was so clear that she could smell the smoke . . .

The hands of the clock crawled round to one o'clock, which meant that there would be no one about for six hours. Looked at from one o'clock in the morning, the night stretched endlessly ahead.

She shut her eyes again and tried not to think about buttered toast and mugs of milky cocoa. She opened them quickly when the door opened and the professor walked in.

Anyone else would have said unnecessarily, 'Awake?' She was immensely cheered when he asked, 'Hungry?' and came to stand by the bed, looking down at her.

She nodded. 'Oughtn't you to be in bed?' she asked.

He sat down on the bed. 'I had to go to a very dull dinner party, and then I had some letters to write. I'm hungry, too. How about some sandwiches and a drink? Cocoa, tea, milk?'

'Cocoa, please.'

He said, to her surprise, 'I'm a dab hand at sandwiches. Give me ten minutes.'

He was very soon back, carrying a tray with mugs of cocoa and a plate piled high with sandwiches. He put it down on the bedside table and handed her a mug, and when she had drunk some of it he took it from her and put a sandwich into her hand. 'Chicken,' he told her, and took one himself, pulled up a chair and sat down. 'Are you very wide awake?'

'Yes.' She spoke thickly through the sandwich.

'Good. Listen to me. You will stay here tomorrow; you can't get a job until your hand is better, and it will give you time to decide what you want to do. If you're dead set on training as a nurse, I'll see what I can do, though I don't think it's the life for you.'

'Would I be a better teacher? Some small school . . .'

'It needs careful thought,' he said smoothly. 'I think the best plan is for you to go and stay with my aunts and think about it—after all, it is your whole future—you don't want a dead-end job.'

'But I can't go there.' She accepted another sandwich and took a bite.

'They will be glad to have you, and you can make yourself useful, picking up balls of wool, and finding their spectacles. They liked you.'

'You are very kind, but I can't impose on them, or you. I'm so sorry it's always you who finds me.' She finished the sandwich and he offered her the mug again, and she finished its contents down to the last drop.

'Your hand is hurting?'

'Well, yes, but it's better now that I'm not hungry.' She had a third sandwich in her hand, but with it half-way to her mouth put it down again. 'I feel sleepy . . .'

The professor put down the plate and picked up the mug and studied its emptiness with satisfaction, and she muttered, 'You put something in my cocoa.'

'Naturally I did. You need a night's dreamless sleep. Goodnight, Suzannah.'

She closed her eyes, mumbled something and fell deeply asleep.

He picked up the tray and stood looking at her. Her face was still pale, but her newly washed hair gave it a glow. She looked a great deal better than she had when he had found her at the hospital; all the same, there was nothing about her ordinary face to attract a man's attention. He shrugged his massive shoulders and took the tray downstairs and went to his bed.

He was up early, for he was operating that morning, and he and his senior registrar would hold outpatients in the late afternoon, but before he left the house he went to the kitchen where he spent ten minutes talking to Mrs Cobb.

'You just leave it to me, sir,' she told him. 'I'll pop along to Harrods and get all the young lady needs. A size ten, I should think; just a slip of a thing, she is.'

'I'll leave the matter in your capable hands, Mrs Cobb, but I beg of you, choose nothing brown or grey . . .'

'A pretty blue or green, sir.'

When he had left the house and Cobb had come back into the kitchen, she was at the table making a list. 'Mark my words,' she observed to her husband, 'he doesn't know it yet, but he's sweet on her. She's just right for him, too—she'll make him a good wife. It'll be nice to have children in the house.'

Cobb sat down at the table. 'Running ahead a bit, aren't you, my dear?'

'Maybe I am, but you mark my words . . .'

Presently she took up a splendid breakfast to Suzannah, sat her up against her pillows, and advised her to stay in bed for a while. 'I'll be back presently with some clothes for you, Miss Lightfoot, and give you a hand with a bath. You mustn't get that hand wet. The professor left some tablets for you; you're to take them if you have any pain.' She beamed at Suzannah. 'Now I'll be off and see what I can find for you to wear.'

'I haven't any money,' said Suzannah.

'Don't worry about that. You'll get compensation.'

Mrs Cobb had gone before Suzannah could ask any more questions, so she went to sleep again.

She woke up to see Mrs Cobb standing by her bed, bearing a small tray daintily laid with cup and saucer, small coffee-pot, cream and sugar.

'There, you've had a nice sleep. Just you drink your coffee while I show you the things I've bought.' She beamed with pleasure as she laid her shopping on the bed. 'Size ten—I checked; I told the professor that's what you'd be, so small you are.' She gave a glance of good-humoured envy at Suzannah's person, enveloped in one of Mrs Cobb's voluminous nighties.

There were undies: scraps of silk and lace in pale colours, the sort of garments Suzannah had drooled over when she had had occasion to go to the shops. There was a skirt, tweed, in a glowing blue-green, and a matching sweater, a couple of ivory silk shirts and a thick tweed top coat in a shade just a little darker than the skirt. There were shoes too, and a pair of slippers as well as a quilted dressing-gown.

Suzannah looked at them all in amazement, and then with regret. 'But I can't wear these,' she pointed out. 'I haven't a penny to my name; besides, I've never had anything like them. Even if I had some money, I doubt if it would be enough . . .'

'Now you're not to worry your head, Miss Lightfoot. The professor said you were to be fitted out so's you can go to his aunts for a few days, just while you get over that nasty fire. He said Harrods, and it's more than my job's worth not to do as he says.'

She saw Suzannah's questioning look. 'Not but he isn't the kindest man on this earth, but when he wants something done, then it's done, if you see what I mean.'

'Yes,' Suzannah almost wailed, 'but I can't take clothes from someone I hardly know.'

'Well, you can't stay in bed for ever, love, can you? Nor can you leave this place mother-naked. Your own clothes were in a fine state, past cleaning and mending, and I don't suppose that you noticed that you'd lost a shoe.'

'Did I? To whom do I go, I wonder, to find out about my clothes and things?'

'I'd leave that for the professor,' advised Mrs Cobb comfortably.

So presently Suzannah got up, had a bath and with Mrs Cobb's help got into her new clothes. Everything fitted, even the shoes, and when Mrs Cobb sat her down in front of the triple mirror on the dressing-table and brushed her hair smooth and tied it back with a blue ribbon Suzannah heaved a great sigh. 'Clothes make a difference, don't they?'

'Indeed they do, miss, and the colour's just right for you, with that hair. Cobb will have lunch ready for you downstairs if you would like to come down.'

So Suzannah went downstairs to eat her lunch under Cobb's fatherly eye, and then sit in the drawing-room with Henry and Horace for company. They shared her tea too, and presently Cobb came in to collect the tea-tray and turn on the six o'clock news.

The professor came in half an hour later, so quietly that at first she wasn't aware that he was there, standing just inside the room. It was Henry trotting over to greet him that caused her to turn round and see him there.

He wished her good evening in a cool voice that instantly deflated her, so that she responded shyly and then rushed in with her thanks, getting more and more muddled until he stopped her with a curt, 'Never mind that, Suzannah. I'm glad to see that you are feeling more yourself. My aunts will be delighted to have you to stay for a few days. Cobb shall drive you down tomorrow.'

Which chilling speech, coupled with the fact that he hadn't appeared to notice her new outfit, caused her to retire behind a polite manner which even to her own ears sounded wooden. She sat there, trying to think of some well-turned phrase which would get her out of the room; it seemed obvious to her that, although he had given her shelter and clothes most generously, he had no wish for her company. But when she suggested that she was tired and would go to bed, he sat down opposite her with the quelling observation that it should be possible for them to dine together without the danger of them falling out, at least for an hour or so.

This annoyed her. 'I have no intention of falling out

with you, Professor, you have been very kind to me and I'm grateful, although I must say you have made it very difficult for me to thank you.'

'Have I?' he smiled a little. 'Do the clothes fit?'

She refrained from breaking into a paean of delight about them. 'Perfectly, thank you. If you will let me have the bill, I will pay you back when I get a job.'

He agreed carelessly and got up to get her a drink, but he had barely sat down again when Cobb came in to say that he was wanted on the phone. And when he came back after a few minutes it was to say that he would have to go out again and would probably not be back for dinner. 'So I'll say goodbye, Suzannah. I have asked my aunts' doctor to take a look at that hand, and in the meantime you can decide what you want to do.'

She stared at him. How on earth was she to get a job, or even start looking for one, without a penny in the world? She hadn't the price of a stamp, let alone the money to take her to any interview she might be lucky enough to get. She had an urge to fling herself on to his great chest and tell him that, but all she did was sit very upright in her chair and wish him goodbye in a quiet voice.

It took her completely by surprise when he came over to her chair and bent and kissed her quite savagely before he went.

'Well,' said Suzannah, and, since she was bereft of words, 'Well, whatever next?' The answer to the question came out of the blue to shock her. There would be nothing next; he didn't like her, he found her a nuisance, and it was his misfortune that she invariably ended up on his doorstep. And, far worse, she had fallen in love with him. 'And I can't think why,' she told

Horace and Henry, for she had to tell someone and there was no one else there. 'He's tiresome and ill-tempered and impatient, and he must hate the sight of me.'

A good cry would have been a comfort, but Cobb came in then to tell her that dinner was waiting, so she went to the dining-room and ate her lonely meal, choking down tears with the delicious food, and presently, with the plea that she was tired, she went to bed.

'What time do we go in the morning?' she asked Cobb as she wished him goodnight.

'We're to be there for lunch, miss. If we leave around ten o'clock, that should give us plenty of time. Mrs Cobb's found a case for the rest of your things, and we wondered about Horace . . . ?'

'Oh, do you suppose that Lady Manbrook would mind if I took him with me? I expect I'll have that little flat again . . .'

'I couldn't say, miss, but I'm sure no one would object to Horace—a well-behaved cat.'

'Yes, he's a great comfort to me. Thank you and Mrs Cobb for looking after him so very well.'

'A pleasure, miss. Henry will miss him.'

She went upstairs to bed and lay thinking about the future. Something domestic, she decided, for there was always work for such; for the moment she would have to give up her idea about training as a nurse. First she must save some money and find herself and Horace somewhere to live as quickly as possible. It was kind of Lady Manbrook to have her, but she had no intention of staying a day longer than she had to. She was already beholden to the professor, and she wanted to get away from him as soon as possible. Out of sight, out of mind, she told herself, and burst into tears at the thought of never seeing him again. Somehow that mattered far more than her precarious future.

CHAPTER EIGHT

LONG before Suzannah went downstairs the next morning, the professor had left his house. She ate the breakfast set before her, gathered Horace into his basket, and, when Cobb had put her few possessions into the boot, got into the car beside him.

The journey was uneventful and rather silent. Suzannah discussed the weather at length, the state of the road and the perfection of Mrs Cobb's cooking, but presently she fell silent and Cobb, beyond the odd word now and then, didn't disturb her.

She thought it unlikely that she would see the professor again; he had wished her goodbye without expressing any hope that he might meet her in the future, and although the thought of never seeing him again was almost too much to bear, she intended to do her utmost to avoid that happening. Unkind fate had thrown her into his path and he had been too kind to ignore her; all the same, she guessed that he must be heartily sick of seeing her. Once she was at Lady Manbrook's house she would contrive to phone Mrs Coffin and persuade her to write and beg her to go to her—a broken arm, flu, varicose veins? thought Suzannah wildly; anything which would make it necessary for Mrs Coffin to call upon her for help. Once there, she could set about finding a job, preferably miles away where she was unlikely to encounter the professor ever again. She had it all most nicely sorted out in her head by the time they reached Ramsbourne House, so that she was able to wish Cobb a cheerful goodbye and greet her hostess with calm.

Lady Manbrook and Mrs van Beuck welcomed her warmly, expressed their admiration of her conduct at the fire, commiserated with her over her burnt hand and hoped that she would stay for as long as she wished.

'And you have brought your cat with you? He won't mind being in the house? We have given you a room with a balcony, so that he may feel free to take the air.'

Parsons took her upstairs presently, to a charming room overlooking the grounds at the back of the house. 'It's nice to see you again, miss,' said Parsons. 'We're all so sorry that you burnt your hand. The ladies were ever so upset.'

She tweaked the bedspread into exactitude, put Suzannah's small bag on the low chest by the closet and went away.

Suzannah took off her coat, tidied her hair and examined her room, while Horace explored his territory, decided on the most comfortable chair, and curled up and went to sleep, leaving her to go downstairs to the drawing-room to drink a glass of sherry with the old ladies before lunch.

She had no opportunity to telephone Mrs Coffin that day, nor the following day either; it would have been simple enough to walk to the village, she supposed, and phone from there, but she had no money and for the moment she had no idea how to get any. She spent the next day or two devising ways and means of getting hold of even a few coins, enough even for a stamp, but none of them were sensible enough to carry out. And she had nothing to sell . . .

Life was pleasant at Ramsbourne House, slow-moving, gracious living which was very soothing. Suzannah's pale cheeks were pale no longer, her hand healed, even her hair seemed to glow more brightly, but it couldn't last, she told herself. In two days' time, she promised herself, she would talk to Lady Manbrook and explain, and ask her if she could borrow some money from her. But first she would try and telephone; she was sure that Mrs Coffin, once she had understood how Suzannah was placed, would help.

The professor had had a busy week which perhaps accounted for his slightly testy manner and his thoughtful silences. Mrs Cobb, noticing this, nodded her head in satisfaction, pointing out to Cobb that she had told him so, hadn't she?

To which he replied that she was fancying things, for the professor had given no hint that he intended seeing Miss Lightfoot again. Which was true, although he had thought about her a great deal; not very willingly, it had to be said, but her small image frequently danced before his eyes, reminding him that even though she wasn't in his house, she had left something of herself behind. It had been with difficulty that he had refrained from telephoning his aunts to find out how she was, but he had eventually decided to wait for at least two weeks, and in the meantime he would see about finding her a job. There was no reason why he should do that, but the thought of her struggling to start all over again was a continuous nagging worry to him. He sat at his desk, considering what he should do; probably, he told himself with a shrug, he would end up with Horace back with Mrs Cobb and Suzannah at the other end of the country. He frowned, for the idea didn't appeal to him.

He looked at the papers on his desk waiting for his attention and then ignored them, deep in thought and only disturbed when Cobb tapped on the door, but before he could speak he was pushed aside and Phoebe went past him to fling herself at the professor.

'Guy—darling—it's ages since I saw you last. I'm in town to do some shopping and I thought we might go out—take me out to dinner, will you?' She jerked her head at a disapproving Cobb, still standing in the doorway. 'He said you were busy, but you're never too busy to see little me, are you?'

The professor had got to his feet. 'It's all right, Cobb,' he said, and pulled up a chair for his visitor. 'This is a surprise, Phoebe. I'm afraid it's out of the question to take you out, though. I've a backlog of work which simply has to be done.'

She pouted prettily. 'Oh, Guy—and I was certain you'd give me dinner.' She saw his bland face and changed her tactics. 'Well, anyway, I'll give you all the news. Uncle keeps fit enough, I suppose, though I'm sure he'd be glad to see you—you must come down for a weekend soon. I've made quite a few changes, too. Old Toms doesn't approve, but who cares what he thinks? We need someone younger in his place; I'll be glad when I can find an excuse to get rid of him. Which reminds me—I saw something on the television about a fire in a kids' nursery school and that red-haired girl I sacked was on the screen with some woman or other. So she fell on her feet, didn't she? Her sort always do.'

The professor had no comment to make upon this, and Phoebe rattled on, 'I must say she looked positively dowdy.'

The professor leaned back in his chair and put his hands in his pockets. 'I dare say she did. She had just been back into the fire to rescue a small boy. Her hand was burned and I found her at the hospital waiting to have it dressed.'

'You saw her?' Phoebe said quickly. 'How interesting.'

'Not interesting; pathetic if you like, and extraordinary.' He ignored her sharp look. 'She is at present staying with Lady Manbrook until she is quite well again.'

He had spoken very quietly, but something in his voice made her frown. She said lightly, 'You sound quite concerned about her; after all, she's only a girl from the village.'

He said evenly, 'A rather special girl, Phoebe. And now, if you will excuse me, I really have to work.'

She flounced off her chair, stood up, opened the door and saw him rise to see her to his front door. She stood a minute, looking at him, conjuring up a smile. 'Well, I hope she gets well soon and finds a decent job. I expect meeting her unexpectedly like that was a bit of a surprise. It sounds very romantic, plunging back into the fire, and actually saving the child; no wonder you think she's a bit special . . .'

But, although she smiled, her eyes were cold. She didn't make the mistake of kissing him, but offered a hand and said cheerfully, 'Don't forget to visit Uncle William some time—bye for now.'

There was a cruising taxi passing; the professor lifted an arm, crossed the pavement with her and saw her into it, and then went back to his desk. He sat there—making no attempt to work—and presently, when

Cobb came to tell him that dinner was served, he wandered into the dining-room and sat down while Cobb handed him his soup.

'I'll be away this weekend, Cobb,' he said presently. 'I'm spending it with Lady Manbrook.'

A titbit of news Cobb lost no time in conveying to his wife.

The professor drove himself down on Saturday morning under a lowering February sky and in the teeth of a howling wind. He had decided to break his journey and lunch on the way, for he remembered that his aunts were in the habit of taking a nap after that meal, which meant that Suzannah would probably be alone. He wasn't at all sure why he was so anxious to see her; she was, he supposed, on his conscience, and for some reason he felt bound to do something about her future.

Snow opened the door to him, took his coat, mentioned that his aunts were resting and in their rooms, but that Miss Lightfoot was in the drawing-room and ushered him across the hall.

'I'll see myself in,' said the professor, and opened the door and walked without haste into the room.

Suzannah was sitting by the fire with Horace on her lap, her head full of ideas and plans, none of which were of any use unless she had some money. She turned round as the door opened to see who it was, and when she saw the professor said what was uppermost in her mind.

'Would you lend me a pound?'

If he was surprised, he didn't show it; his lip twitched briefly but his voice was quite steady. 'Of course.' He fished around among his loose change and offered two coins. 'Though I think two pounds would be more sensible, you might lose one.'

'I'll pay you back as soon as I've found a job.' She saw his faint smile and blushed. 'I'm sorry, you must think I'm mad, but I was thinking that if I had some money I could telephone, or take a bus or something; you have no idea how awkward it is when one hasn't a penny piece in the world.'

'My fault—I overlooked that fact when you came here. I do apologise.'

'Oh, I'm not blaming you, indeed I'm not, you've done so much for me and really it must be so vexing for you, my always turning up to annoy you.'

He came and sat down opposite her. 'But you don't annoy me, Suzannah; indeed I find that I miss you . . .'

A great surge of love threatened to explode in her chest, but she kept a calm face. 'Well, perhaps you do, like missing an aching tooth!'

He laughed. 'You're happy here? I see that your hand is better. If you will be patient for a little longer, I will see what I can do about getting you into a teaching hospital where you can live out.'

As he spoke, he was aware that he had no intention of doing any such thing; he badly wanted to have a finger in the pie when it came to her future.

He hadn't expected her refusal. 'That's awfully kind of you, but I thought I'd get some kind of domestic work in the country; I'd quite like to go to Scotland, or if there's nothing for me there, Yorkshire. Somewhere miles away.'

He was astonished at the wave of dismay that swept through him at the news. 'A long way for Horace,' was all he said.

'Yes, but once we're there we'd stay.'

He said evenly, 'So you want to start again, Suzannah? A new life with new surroundings and new friends?'

She nodded. 'Yes, oh, yes, you have no idea how much I want to do that.'

The professor looked at her, sitting neatly opposite him, hands folded over Horace's furry body; certainly no beauty, but possessed of something most of the women of his acquaintance didn't have—charm and a certain kind of gentleness which masked a sturdy independence. And the most beautiful eyes he had ever seen. He had been tolerably satisfied with his life until now, but he knew that that wasn't true any longer. Life wouldn't be the same if Suzannah were to go away; what he had supposed had been concern for a girl who had been left to fend for herself had evidently developed into something else, something he wasn't going to put a name to until he was sure, and it looked as though he would have no need to do that, for she had spoken with a quiet conviction; she wanted to go away, a long way away, too, and seeing him again hadn't entered into her head.

He was a patient man and he had made up his mind; moreover, he liked to get his own way. He said smoothly, 'Now, let me see, I should think somewhere like York would suit you admirably—do you know the city?'

He began to talk effortlessly about that part of England, never mentioning her future; he was still chatting idly when the old ladies joined them and they had tea, talking of other things.

Suzannah, in her room, doing her face and hair before dinner, told herself that he really had no interest in her, only a polite concern, and as for his coming for the weekend, probably he did that regularly. It was heavenly to see him again, but she must get away before he came again or offered to find her work. If she were several hundred miles away, life would be so much easier. She didn't believe that, but it sounded sensible.

The evening passed pleasantly enough. The old ladies discussed art, the repairs to the church and if it would be possible to have the tapestry curtains in the small sitting-room repaired by an expert. The professor took a polite interest, while sitting watching Suzannah, his mind on other things, and presently, while they were having their coffee, he invited her with just the right amount of casualness to accompany him the next morning to his house. 'I need to check on the barn roof,' he explained, 'and it will be a pleasant drive even in February.'

It would have seemed strange for her to refuse. She agreed calmly and asked where he lived. 'I thought your home was in London?'

'Well, it is, but my home—where I was born, is at Great Chisbourne, on the edge of the Savernake Forest. I think you may like it.'

She would have liked a two-up and two-down with no mod. cons. if he had lived in it; but she said politely, 'I'm sure I shall.'

They left after breakfast, a meal at which the professor had chatted about this and that without saying anything to the point, while eating with a splendid appetite. Suzannah, a prey to a fine muddle of thoughts, did her best with her scrambled eggs, crumbled toast and drank several cups of coffee while making polite replies when necessary. She was in a state of euphoria at the very idea of spending several hours with the professor, so that she was a trifle absent-minded.

The weather had shown little improvement since the previous day and there was little traffic; the professor drove fast, slowing down to go through Marlborough and then turning on to a side road which led them through the centre of the forest, until the trees thinned and they reached Great Chisbourne, a small village with the forest at its back and rolling country beyond. The main street was wide and lined with nice old houses, and at its end the professor turned the car through an open gateway and stopped before the house at the end of the short drive.

It was of a comfortable size, of mellow red brick, and with an ancient slate roof which rose in a series of irregular gables, interspersed with tall, elaborate chimneys. It stood in large grounds with trees grouped behind it and a grass lawn before it, ringed around with flower-beds; even on such a dull day, it looked charming.

Suzannah went with the professor to his front door, which was opened as they reached it by a small dumpling of a woman with white hair and black beady eyes. He greeted her with a hug and a kiss and turned to Suzannah.

'This is Trudy, my old nanny; she lives here and looks after me when I come here.'

Suzannah shook hands, conscious that she was being studied closely, but not, she thought, unkindly.

'There's coffee waiting,' said Trudy. 'I'll show you where you can put your coat, Miss Lightfoot, and you, Mr Guy, be sure and hang yours up in the closet.'

Suzannah was borne away and shown a well-appointed cloakroom at the back of the hall, and presently returned to find the professor lounging on the gilt and marble table standing against one wall of the hall, his hands in his pockets, whistling. The hall was warm and welcoming and had wood-panelled walls and a polished floor with thick Turkish carpet down its centre. There were high-backed, rush-seated chairs on either side of the table, which held a great bowl of hyacinths, and wall sconces with mulberry silk shades. A pleasing sight, although it was the sight of the professor which pleased her most.

The room which they went into was long, reaching from the front of the house to the back, with a low-beamed ceiling, a huge fireplace and bay windows at each end. The floor was as highly polished as the hall and strewn with silky rugs in faded jewel colours, which were reflected in the swathed curtains at the windows. The furniture was a pleasing blend of comfortable arm-chairs and sofas and much polished dark oak. There were wall sconces here too, capped in ivory silk, and some splendid paintings in elaborate gilt frames, mostly portraits. Suzannah hoped that she might have the chance later of inspecting them.

They sat by the log fire and drank their coffee, the dog between them, and once again the professor didn't allow the conversation to stray from general topics. Perhaps that was just as well, reflected Suzannah, for otherwise she might find herself saying more than she meant. But even so she was enjoying herself; she was discovering that when the professor was there nothing else seemed to matter; the fact that she had no money, no clothes and a hazardous future seemed unimportant.

She decided, as she sat there, that she would enjoy every minute of the day and never mind anything else.

Presently he fetched their drinks from the Jacobean oak court cupboard before, at Trudy's invitation they crossed the hall to have their lunch. The dining-room was furnished in the Stuart style, with a long side-table, its burr-walnut inlaid with floral marquetry, the chairs around the table elegant William and Mary. There were long crimson curtains at the windows and above the fireplace was a wooden carving of fruit and flowers. Suzannah paused to look at it. 'That looks like Grinling Gibbons,' she ventured.

'Well, I hope so, since he carved it.' He smiled at her. 'Come and sit down and let us see what Trudy has got for us.'

Trudy, besides being a nanny, was an exceptional cook; no frills, no *nouvelle cuisine*, but little cheese soufflés for starters, followed by steak and kidney pudding, properly made with oysters and mushrooms and accompanied by boiled potatoes and sprouts, and for a pudding a bread and butter pudding which qualified as ambrosia.

· 'I dare say you come here as often as you can,' observed Suzannah, as she poured their coffee.

The professor had watched her tucking in to the good food with hidden delight. 'Indeed, yes. When I marry I shall make a point of coming here each weekend; this is, after all, my home, and I should like my children to grow up here.'

She was just a little bit muzzy from the sherry and the wine. 'You are going to marry, Professor?'

'Certainly. Would you like to see the gardens before it becomes too dark?'

And if that wasn't a snub, she reflected, what was?

She got her coat and they went through a door at the back of the hall, into a glassed-in patio which in turn led to the gardens beyond. Even in mid-winter they were a delight: narrow paths bordered by shrubs and trees, a gazebo at the end of a long walk edged with flower-beds which in the summer would be a blaze of colour.

'You like it?' asked the professor.

'It's heaven,' declared Suzannah. 'I don't know how you can bear to be away from it.'

'I am able to come for most weekends,' he pointed out. 'We aren't far from the motorway, you know, it's a quick run up to town.'

She was dying to ask him if he would drive up to town each day—surely not?—or live in London during the week and rejoin his family at weekends. He must have read her mind, for he said idly, 'Of course, my wife and children would have to divide their time between London and here . . .'

'Yes, but when they start going to school,' she pointed out seriously.

'Ah, then I should have to commute.' He smiled at her. 'There's a charming little pond at the end of the garden; shall we have a look at it?'

He wasn't going to allow her to see into his private life. She went rather red at the idea of prying into it. She said briefly, 'I'd like to see it. How big is your garden?'

'About four acres—there's a kitchen garden and a small orchard beyond.' He took her arm. 'There's a paddock, too. There are a couple of worn-out donkeys there; no one wanted them, so they live out their elderly lives here . . .'

'Oh, how nice. Will they do for the children when

you have them?'

'Admirably. You are not bored with my aunts, Suzannah?'

'Bored? Goodness, no. It's heaven, not having anything to bother one, you know. But now I have some money I shall go into Marlborough and get the papers and find work.'

He came to a halt, and still he was holding her arm, so she stopped too. 'Ah, yes, I was wondering if you could see your way to staying at Ramsbourne House for a little longer; I believe that I know of something which might suit you.'

The last thing she wanted. Especially if it were to be near his home. She must get away at all costs. She said, 'I really had made up my mind to go right away from here.'

'Why?'

She went rather pale. 'Well . . . it would make a nice change.'

'You have a reason,' his voice was very even, 'but you don't want to tell me, do you, Suzannah?'

'No. No, I don't, if you don't mind.'

He nodded and started to walk on again. 'Shall we go and take a look at the donkeys?'

'Yes, please. Who looks after them when you're not here?'

'Trudy's nephew. She was born and brought up in the village, and most of her family have looked after us. She never married, but she has three sisters and any number of nephews and nieces; they run my home between them.'

He opened a wicket gate at the end of the path and entered the paddock. There was a large shed at its farther end, and along one outside edge was a high brick wall, crowned with tiles. He nodded towards this. 'The kitchen garden is on the other side; that leads to the back yard and the garages. That roof you can see is the barn; we'll take a look at it presently.'

The donkeys were in the shed, standing contentedly side by side. They were elderly but well cared for, and ambled over to meet them as they went in. The professor reached up to a wooden box on a ledge above his head and pulled out a handful of carrots. 'This one's Joe—the one who is eating your carrots is Josephine.'

They stayed a little while with the gentle beasts, and then crossed the paddock and went through a narrow wooden door into the kitchen garden, walled and sheltered, with peach and pear and nectarine trees against the red brick. There was a greenhouse, too, with a vine wreathed around its walls. 'Been there for ages, long before my time,' observed the professor. 'We get good grapes from it.'

The garden was a model of orderliness, with rows of cauliflowers and winter cabbage, leeks and Brussels sprouts and, under cloches along one wall, neat rows of seedlings. The professor took his time looking at everything which rather surprised Suzannah; it seemed to her that he had enough on his hands, operating and presiding over out-patients and checking on his patients in the wards. She asked, 'Don't you get tired? I mean, you have a busy week at the hospital, I expect, and then you come down here . . .'

'Ah, but you see, this is my real life. I love my work, but I believe that I am a country man at heart. I count myself very fortunate that I have the best of both worlds.'

They wandered out of the kitchen garden and into the yard behind the house, and he inspected the barn roof and then took her back into the house through the back door.

It was getting dark already; there were lights into the stone passage which led to the hall. He took her coat and Trudy came from the kitchen with the tea tray.

'Muffins, Mr Guy,' she told him as she went past, 'and a nice chocolate cake I made this morning, seeing that you were coming. There's sandwiches with Gentleman's Relish, and some nice thin bread and butter.'

Suzannah, sitting by the fire again, could think of no way better to spend a winter's afternoon than by a blazing fire, eating muffins and listening to the professor talking about nothing in particular.

She sat, looking into the flames and wishing she could stay forever, envying from the bottom of her heart the girl she thought he was going to marry. She took a quick peep at him, sitting there, his long legs stretched out before him, the dog with his head at his master's feet. In the firelight he was better-looking than ever. She remembered the first time she had met him and his cold stare . . . He looked up and the stare wasn't cold now; indeed, it caused her to frown a little, so that he said casually, 'I suppose we must think about going back to the aunts. They expect us for dinner.'

She got up with the vague feeling that he had been going to say something else and then changed his mind. 'I've had a lovely day; thank you very much for inviting me.'

He went unhurriedly to the door and held it open. 'I shall be coming down again very shortly: I promised

Phoebe that I would take a look at Sir William; she seemed rather worried about him. She asked after you, by the way.'

Suzannah was surprised. 'Did she?' She sought for something suitable to say. 'That was very kind of her.'

'Possibly,' said the professor, and followed her into the hall.

He left Ramsbourne House very shortly after dinner that evening. He had wished his aunts goodbye and then invited Suzannah to see him out of the house. She went with him, thinking that perhaps she wouldn't see him again, for she fully intended to be away before he came again. At the door he turned her round to face him, his hands on her shoulders.

'Next time I come we will settle your future, once and for all. No more jobs which lead nowhere—something permanent.'

He bent and kissed her hard, and was gone before she could utter a sound.

His kiss shook her badly, so that she didn't remember his words until some time in the middle of the night. Something permanent, he had said, but perhaps it would be somewhere she would see him, and that was something she was determined not to do, not even if it was only on rare occasions. He had mentioned training as a nurse and probably he had spoken to someone at his own hospital where his word was taken heed of, and that wouldn't do at all. 'I must make a clean break,' she told a drowsy Horace, and then lay awake until it was getting light, wondering how best to do it.

She had had an almost sleepless night for nothing, for fate had taken a hand again. It was the following afternoon while the old ladies were taking their post-prandial nap that Suzannah was sitting in the drawing-room writing out an advert to put in *The Lady* magazine and another one for the local weekly paper, made possible by fifty pounds in the envelope Snow had handed her that morning with the murmured observation that the professor had asked him to let Suzannah have it when she came downstairs. There was a scrawled note with the money, begging her to accept it, 'just to tide you over; you can repay me later.'

She had been reluctant to accept it, but with money she could do so much more, not only advertise but travel to interviews should they be forthcoming.

She was making a fair copy when Snow came soft-footed into the room. 'Miss Davinish has called, miss. She would like to see you; I told her that the ladies were resting, but she said she had come to see you.'

'Me?' Suzannah jumped up in surprise. Perhaps Miss Davinish wanted her back—perhaps the cottage was vacant again and she could go there to live, only she couldn't: it was too near the professor's home . . . 'Thank you, Snow; would you ask her to come in? Lady Manbrook wouldn't mind?'

'Certainly not, miss. She is acquainted with Miss Davinish.'

Phoebe Davinish came into the room with an air of being entirely at home there. She stood for a moment just inside the door, studying Suzannah, who was standing uncertainly by the table. She said, 'Hello. I'm on my way home and it seemed a good opportunity to see you.' She sat down and undid her fur coat. 'I dare say you're wondering why I've called to see you?'

'Yes, I am rather.'

Phoebe smiled as she watched her. 'Did Guy—

Professor Bowers-Bentinck come to see you this weekend?'

'Not me specially. He came to visit his aunts.'

Phoebe went on smoothly, 'Oh, I understood him to say that he would be seeing you. He's concerned about you; thinks you should have a chance to get a permanent job . . .'

She paused to watch Suzannah's reaction and smiled when she replied, 'Well, yes, he did say that he would like me to stay here, as he thought he knew of something . . .'

Pheobe went on chattily. 'Did he tell you that we are to be married?' She paused again and watched the colour leave Suzannah's cheeks. 'I see that he didn't. Well, I can understand that—you do show your feelings rather openly, and he does dislike hurting people's feelings.'

Suzannah thought wildly that that didn't sound like the professor at all; he was kind, certainly, but quite ruthless about getting his own way. But she said nothing, sitting there listening to Phoebe whom she knew didn't like her, but who sounded so plausible now.

'Well, we have had a splendid idea. We shall need more staff, of course; I suggested that you might like to come as Girl Friday—you know, answer the phone, write letters, take calls for Guy, help around the house. You would have a room to yourself, of course, and wages . . .'

So that was the permanent job he had had in mind, thought Suzannah, and anything less possible she had yet to think of. She wished very much that she could scream with rage and misery and throw something at the girl sitting opposite her, but instead she said in a calm voice, 'That's very kind of you, Miss Davinish. It's rather a surprise, and not quite what I had planned to do . . .'

'Oh and what was that?'

Phoebe sounded quite friendly; everything was going very nicely. She had banked on Suzannah's refusing; she wasn't the kind of girl to let a man know that she was in love with him—she would want to put the whole of England between them.

'I mean to go right away, and as soon as possible.'

'Well, I dare say that might be a good idea, after all, although I'm sure Guy will want to help in any way he can. You'll need money.'

Suzannah thought of the fifty pounds. 'I think I can manage.'

Phoebe started to do up her coat.

'Well, do let us know if you need help. Guy is a great one for helping lame dogs over stiles, you know.'

She got to her feet and Suzannah got up too and put Horace on the floor. He had been staring unwinkingly at Phoebe; now he crossed the space between them and sank his claws into her coat, and then drew a vicious claw down her tights, ripping them neatly.

Phoebe whirled round and aimed a blow at him, although he had prudently retired under the table by then. 'You damned brute,' she screamed, 'you've ruined my tights and probably my coat as well! You're dangerous——' She glared at Suzannah. 'You should have him put down . . . You'll pay for this.'

She stormed out, brushing past an astonished Snow and banging the front door behind her, and he returned to the drawing-room to ask, 'What was all that about, miss?'

'Horace scratched her, Snow.' Suzannah had stopped to pick up Horace who looked as though butter wouldn't melt in his mouth. 'She said he should be put down.'

Snow's stern face relaxed very slightly. 'A more docile beast I have yet to meet, miss. A very nice cat, if I may say so.'

When he had gone, Suzannah sat down again with Horace on her knee. She said softly, 'I don't blame you, Horace; if I had claws I would have done exactly the same.'

He settled down, purring loudly, and when he felt the top of his head getting damp from her tears he took no notice.

CHAPTER NINE

THERE was time for Suzannah to go to the village and post her letters off to the magazine and newspaper she had chosen. She left Horace snoozing before the fire, got her outdoor things, and walked briskly to the general stores with its additional small sub-post-office. The shop was full, and only Mrs Maddox who owned it was there to serve, discussing the merits of streaky bacon with a customer. Suzannah wandered over to the corner where the newspapers and a variety of magazines were on display, and picked up the morning's paper. She put it down again as her eye lighted on the board hanging on the wall behind the paper stand. It was full of cards: local teenagers wanted to pick watercress, a carrycot for sale, kittens wanting good homes, charming widow in her forties would like to meet a friendly gentleman of a similar age for outings, and then, wedged in among the prams, kitchen tables and winter coats on offer was something Suzannah felt was meant for her. It was written in black ink and heavily underlined. Strong young woman required at once to assist in moving family to York. Emergency post, temporary until nanny has recovered from illness. To be responsible for two small children and a baby. There was a phone number and an address in Avebury.

Suzannah wasted no time. She was across the street and in the telephone box as fast as her legs would carry her, only once there she remembered that she hadn't any small change. A precious ten minutes was wasted while she went back to the shop and wheedled the queue to let her get change from Mrs Maddox, but finally she got through to Mrs Coffin. That lady listened to what she had to say, and then stayed silent for so long that Suzannah was dancing with impatience. Finally, she said in her comfortable country voice, 'All right, love. If you get this job I'll have Horace; just so long as it's not for more than a week or two.'

Suzannah let out a sigh of relief, thanked her old friend and then dialled the number on the card. A distraught voice answered, and when she asked if the post had been filled, the owner of the voice broke into a long speech in which the baby being sick, the two children making off with a cake cook had just made and the removal men due to arrive the next morning, were jumbled together in a mournful diatribe. Suzannah waited for a pause. 'Then may I come and see you? Perhaps I might do if there is no one else?'

'When can you come?'

Suzannah peered across the street at the church clock. 'Well, I'm not sure about buses, I'm at Ramsbourne St Michael . . .'

'I'll send the gardener to fetch you. Where are you?'

Suzannah told her. 'But I'm afraid I must ask to be brought back here again.'

'That's fine. He'll be along in a few minutes. It's only a mile or two.'

The gnarled old man who drove up presently in a Land Rover had little to say, although he wasn't unfriendly. He turned off the road about a mile out of the village, down a lane full of pot-holes and then in through an open gate to stop before a rambling house; there were no curtains at the windows and the front door was open even on such a cold day. A skip half-full with odds and ends of broken furniture and rubbish was in the drive, and someone was hammering in a demented fashion.

Suzannah got out, thanked her driver and knocked on the open door.

A voice from somewhere in the house begged her to come in and she threaded her way between packing cases, up-ended chairs and tidy stacks of pictures towards it.

The kitchen: a pleasant, cluttered room, but warm and cosy too and at the moment rather crowded. Two small children were sitting at the table eating their tea, an older woman was at the sink, cleaning vegetables, and the owner of the voice was sitting by the Aga with a baby on her lap.

'Sorry for the mess. We're moving house,' she added quite unnecessarily. 'Of course, Nanny would get measles just when she's most needed. Are you strong? The children are awful. Have you any references? Do you live locally—I don't remember seeing you around? My name's Meredith, by the way. My husband's already at York—we've bought a house there but he can't get back to give me a hand. He doesn't know about Nanny.'

There didn't seem to be any necessity to answer any of this; Suzannah picked up the slice of bread and butter one of the children had hurled on to the floor and waited patiently. When Mrs Meredith stopped talking, she said, 'My name is Lightfoot, Suzannah. I lived for a long time with my aunt near Marlborough. She died recently and I want a temporary post while I decide what to do.'

'When can you come? We move the day after tomorrow. I suppose I must ask you for references.'

Suzannah gave the names of Mrs Coffin and Dr Warren.

'And when could you start?' asked Mrs Meredith again. 'I warn you it will be pretty ghastly—Nanny will be away for two weeks and I'm no good with the children.' She smiled suddenly. 'The pay's quite good, and of course we'll pay your fare back.'

She was a pretty woman, not used, Suzannah guessed, to doing things for herself; she rather liked her. 'If my references are all right, I could come early on the day you move, if that would do?'

'My dear girl, you have no idea what a relief it will be to have someone to look after the children and the baby. Can I phone you?'

Suzannah gave her Mrs Coffin's number; the less Lady Manbrook knew the better, just in case the professor should ask. She didn't like fibbing to the nice old lady, but she couldn't think what else to do if she wanted to disappear completely.

Presently she was driven back by the old gardener and set down outside the telephone box, and during the short journey she had time to reflect upon her good fortune. She had time, too, to worry about the fibs she was going to tell old Lady Manbrook; a truthful girl by nature, she was irked at having to deceive the kind old lady, but she could think of nothing else to do. To get away quickly so that she need not see the professor again was paramount in her mind; a few fibs on the way were inevitable.

She thanked the old man and walked back to Ramsbourne House, and at dinner that evening explained that she would have to leave in the morning to look after an old friend from her village. She spoke uncertainly, but the old ladies put that down to her worry about her friend, and since they were both short-sighted they failed to see the guilt written all over her face.

With her few possessions and Horace in his basket she boarded the bus in the morning after bidding the old ladies goodbye. She had told no one where she was going and no one had asked her; that she came from a village not too far away was common knowledge, but its name had never been mentioned. The bus was half-full and no one on it knew her. She felt more and more secure the nearer she got to Mrs Coffin and the village.

She would only be staying for two days, she told Mrs Coffin, paying that lady the modest sum she asked for her lodging. 'And I'll pay you for Horace's food before I go,' promised Suzannah. 'Mrs Meredith said two weeks at the most, if you don't mind.'

'Lor' bless you, love, of course I don't mind and nor does the dog, though I dare say my Tiger will.' She chuckled easily and went to serve a customer, leaving Suzannah to settle Horace by the fire in the sitting-room and unpack her bag.

She hated saying goodbye to Horace; he had been leading a very unsettled life for the last month or so, and he gave her a reproachful look as she stroked his elderly head. 'Don't you fret,' said Mrs Coffin. 'I'll keep an eye on him, and you'll see, something will turn up for you when you get back.'

Suzannah gave her a hug. 'Don't let anyone know

where I am,' she begged.

'Well, there is no one to ask, is there, love?'

Suzannah bent down to examine a shoe. 'No, of course not.'

This time she was to be picked up in Marlborough, again by the old gardener, who, beyond observing that the house was in a rare pickle and he doubted they'd get away before the following day, only said, 'The missus can't seem to manage without nanny or the master, and them children run wild.'

Hardly an encouraging start, reflected Suzannah, but beggars couldn't be choosers and if she were kept busy for the next couple of weeks she might be able to forget the professor. She had been singularly unsuccessful at that so far.

The house, when she reached it, was in a state of chaos; Mrs Meredith had recruited two women from the village to help get the house emptied, and the elderly woman, the cook, was in the kitchen banging pots and saucepans into wooden chests, declaring that she would give in her notice the moment they got to York. The furniture movers were already busy, tramping to and fro, taking no notice of anyone else, calling cheerfully to each other with a good deal of, 'To you, George, and back to you, Tom,' as they manoeuvred weighty pieces of furniture out of the house and into the van.

Mrs Meredith was in her bedroom, trying to decide what to wear. Her face broke into a wide smile when she saw Suzannah. 'Oh, good, you're here. If you could catch the children and get their outdoor clothes on, and then could you possibly change the baby? Cook's going to make tea for everyone before we go. The men say we'll be there by six o'clock . . .'

'But isn't York about a hundred and eighty miles from here?' Suzannah had a mental picture of the two vans and Mrs Meredith racing up the motorway at seventy miles an hour, and even then they'd never get unloaded before midnight. It was a relief when Mrs Meredith laughed. 'Oh, we shall spend a night on the way. We're going across country to the M1 and spending the night at a small place called Crick just off the motorway. My husband has got rooms for us all at the Post House there. It's about half-way, so we should be in York during the afternoon. My husband will be there to meet us and the men will stay overnight at the local pub.'

She turned away to hold up a pale grey trouser suit. 'This would be sensible to travel in, don't you think? I'll be driving the station wagon, Cook can sit beside me and you and the children can sit in the back.'

Sinking her weary head on to the pillow that night, Suzannah went over the day. They had managed to get away somehow; the vans had lumbered off first and then Mrs Meredith, after a last-minute frantic rush around the house to make sure that everything was gone. She was a good driver and they soon overtook the vans, all of them stopping for lunch at a wayside hotel, where she had been kept busy seeing that the children ate their meal, leading them to and from the loo, feeding the baby and changing it and snatching a quick meal for herself. The baby was a good child and slept peacefully for hours at a stretch, which had left her free to amuse the children, both bored stiff by the afternoon. A brief break for tea and they went on again and came at last to the hotel. Mr Meredith had organised everything very well: instructions had been written down, hotels had been advised of their coming and their rooms were comfortable. Suzannah, with the baby in its carry-cot beside her bed and the door open to the children's room, slept the sleep of someone who had done a hard day's work.

The rest of the journey went well. The worst was over, Mrs Meredith assured her; they would stop for lunch on the way and be at their new home before tea-time. And so they were.

The house was a few miles from York—a converted farmhouse, roomy and pleasant to the eye and set in several acres of ground. There were lights streaming from its windows as they drove up, and Mr Meredith came to meet them. An efficient man, Suzannah guessed, for he had tea organised and a sturdy girl to serve it, and in no time at all the room where the children were to sleep had its essential furniture so that she was able to bath and undress them and bring them their suppers in bed before turning her attention to the baby.

She had had her supper with Cook, and Mr Meredith had thanked her for being of such help to his wife. He was a kind man, a little pompous, but highly successful in life and he was fond of his wife; anyone could see that. It would be nice to be married to someone who doted on you, she mused drowsily, and inevitably thought of the professor.

She had intended to ponder her future during the weeks she would be with the Merediths, but she had little time to think, let alone ponder. The children were endearing, full of spirits and extremely naughty. They disappeared a dozen times a day, hiding in the attics or the enormous cupboards; they fought like two puppies and cried loudly if they were thwarted. It was fortunate that the baby was one of the most placid creatures she had ever encountered. All the same, her days were crammed; there was certainly no time to decide her future.

With the help of curtain hangers, window cleaners, carpet layers and the like, the house was quickly a home. The children had their nursery in one wing of the roomy old house, and since there was a side entrance leading to the back stairs Suzannah saw little of Mrs Meredith, although each evening after the children were in bed and the baby settled until the ten o'clock feed, Suzannah was invited to go downstairs for drinks and dinner. And, by the time she had bidden the Merediths goodnight and gone to her own room, she was too tired to think about anything much. Only the professor, and that was a waste of time, she told herself crossly, when she should be planning what was the best thing to do next. Invariably at this point she fell asleep.

The professor, back home after an urgent summons to go to the Middle East and perform an intricate operation upon the small son of an oil sheikh, picked up the letters waiting for him, exchanged a few words with Cobb and went to his study. Cobb followed him in with the whisky he had asked for and the assurance that Mrs Cobb would have dinner ready within fifteen minutes and retired silently, leaving the professor to glance through his post. There was a letter from Lady Manbrook—he recognised her copperplate handwriting —but before he read it he reached for his appointments book. There were private patients to see at his rooms in the forenoon, and before that a ward round at the hospital as well as an outpatients clinic in the afternoon. He sighed faintly, his mind full of Suzannah whom he wanted to see above all people; she had captured his heart and his mind, and he had to steel himself against getting into his car and going down to his aunt's to see her. He opened the letter; at least he knew where she was until he could be with her again.

No one, watching him reading, would have guessed at the great surge of strong feeling which shook him as he deciphered Lady Manbrook's rambling missive. His face was as calm as it always was, only his mouth had tightened and a muscle twitched in his cheek. He had been mistaken; he no longer knew where Suzannah was, if he was to believe his aunt's gentle regret at her guest's sudden departure, and he had no reason to doubt it. He read the letter once more, sat for a little while deep in thought and once more picked up the telephone. His secretary, Mrs Long, would have left his rooms by now; he phoned her home and she listened to what he had to say.

'Two patients in the forenoon, sir,' she assured him, 'and no one in the afternoon; it's your outpatients in the afternoon and you're operating.'

'I'll see to all those, but rearrange the other appointments for the next two days, will you? I have to go away for a couple of days. There wasn't anything desperately urgent, was there?'

'No, sir. I'll do that—will two days be enough?'

'I'm not sure. I'll keep in touch.'

He rang off and then rang the hospital to talk to his registrar. 'I'll be in tomorrow,' he told him, 'but I shall want you to take over for the next two days after that. Sort it out, will you? I'll give you a ring on the second day.'

Cobb tapped on the door to tell him that dinner was ready and the professor said, 'Cobb, Miss Lightfoot has disappeared. I intend to go down to Great Chisbourne tomorrow evening and stay a couple of days. Will you have a bag packed for me when I get back? And a quick meal?'

Cobb looked shocked. 'Of course, sir. Missing, you say? Such a pleasant, level-headed young lady. Mrs Cobb will be quite upset . . .'

The professor smiled grimly. 'Well, tell her not to get too worried; I intend to find her.'

His day was long and hard; he had bent his powerful brain to the delicate task of removing a blood clot from his patient's brain, examined his two private patients and his ward cases and dealt with a number of out-patients before he finally let himself into his house that evening. The faithful Cobb met him in the hall. 'Mrs Cobb has a light meal ready, sir, and your bag is packed. Is there anything further?'

The professor took off his coat and stretched his great arms. 'No, Cobb, thank you, only phone me if you should get any news—I'll be at Great Chisbourne—if I'm not there, give a message to Trudy, will you?'

He went to his room and showered and changed, ate his meal and was back in his car within the hour.

It was late by the time he reached his house, but on the way he had phoned Trudy and she was there, waiting for him, wrapped in a red woolly dressing-gown, reassuringly matter-of-fact and comforting.

'There's coffee and sandwiches, Mr Guy,' she told him, and, after one look at his tired face, 'You're tired to the bone. Something's wrong, isn't it? And you so happy with that nice young lady . . .'

'The nice young lady has run away, Trudy. I have to find her.' He flung his greatcoat down and sat down at the kitchen table while she poured the coffee.

'Well, of course you do. And I'll be bound she's run away for a good reason. If ever I saw a girl in love . . . of course you'll find her.'

The professor said quite meekly, 'Yes, Trudy. I'll go over to Lady Manbrook's in the morning and find out just what happened.'

'You do that, Mr Guy, but first you're going to have a good night's sleep or you won't have your wits about you in the morning.'

His aunts were delighted to see him; they were also vague, but then they always were. It took time to discover that Suzannah had gone to look after an old friend and had taken Horace with her. 'We're not quite sure why she had to go,' they told him, 'but it seemed to be a matter of extreme urgency, for the dear child left very shortly after she had gone down to the village—you remember, dear?' Lady Manbrook asked her sister. 'It was only ten minutes or so after Phoebe Davinish came to see her—we didn't see her, of course, but Parsons told us and Snow did say that Phoebe left looking put out.'

It wasn't much, but it was a start; the professor stayed a little while with the old ladies and drove himself back to his home. Over his lunch he assessed the information he had gleaned; it was obvious to him that Phoebe had been the cause for Suzannah's sudden flight to heaven knew where.

He drove back to Ramsbourne St Michael after

lunch, parked the car and entered the village stores.
Mrs Maddox was behind the counter, waiting for
customers, and it was here that he had success, for she
remembered Suzannah. 'Lovely red hair,' she observed
chattily, 'though she did look a bit worried. The shop
was full and she was looking at those adverts I keep by
the door. Next time I looked up there she was across the
street, phoning from the box, and presently along comes
the old gardener from Mrs Meredith's and she gets in
and off they go.'

'Did she have a cat basket with her?'

Mrs Maddox looked surprised. 'Oh, no, nothing at
all with her. I didn't see her come back . . .'

'And this Mrs Meredith—where does she live?'

He was given a suspicious look. 'Well, sir, I don't
rightly think I should say, for its none of my business.'

The professor, when called upon, could exert great
charm. 'I'm Lady Manbrook's nephew. I am a friend
of Miss Lightfoot's and I do need to see her as soon as
possible.'

'Oh, well, that's different, sir. Mrs Meredith's gone
—somewhere up north. Wait a minute, I've got the
forwarding address somewhere. They went a week or
more ago, and a fine muddle it was getting them
moved, so I hear from all accounts, Mr Meredith not
being able to come here and direct things and Mrs
Meredith, nice though she is, always up in the clouds,
no method if you see what I mean, as well as two of the
naughtiest children I've ever met and a baby, too. Her
Nanny got the measles and she was at her wit's end for
help . . .' She rummaged around on the shelf behind her
and produced a paper. 'Here we are—everything is to
go to Mr Meredith's place of business for the time being

—I suppose they've not settled in yet—I heard tell that it was a place in the country.'

The professor had listened with patience; he was getting somewhere, but far too slowly for his peace of mind. He thanked Mrs Maddox and got into his car. Mrs Coffin seemed a likely link in the chain. He walked into her little shop and was relieved to see the look of guilty consternation on her face.

'Well,' said Mrs Coffin in an agitated voice, 'fancy seeing you here, sir, however did you . . . ?' She stopped and started again. 'Come to look up Dr Warren, I dare say—he'll be back from his rounds by now.'

'I've come to see you, Mrs Coffin, if you could spare me five minutes?'

She made a great thing of looking up and down the village street. 'Well, sir, it's my busy time . . .' She caught his eye; he was smiling, but there was going to be no putting him off, she could see that.

'Come through into the back room, sir,' she invited him unwillingly, and lifted the counter flap for him to join her.

The little room was crammed with furniture and a bright fire burned in the small grate. An elderly dog sat in front of it, a large black cat sat on one side, and on the other Horace was perched, looking uneasy.

The professor stooped to twiddle his ear. 'Hello, old fellow,' and Horace brightened visibly. 'Yes, all right, I'll take you back with me, we shall be glad to have you with us again.'

Mrs Coffin looked relieved. 'Oh, you've come for Suzannah's cat. She was so worried when she left; you see, she wasn't sure how long she would be gone, and him and my Tiger don't get on, only there wasn't anywhere else to take him.'

'That was very kind of you, Mrs Coffin,' said the professor smoothly. 'If you will let me have her address, I'll let Suzannah know that he's back with me.'

'I've got the address somewhere—sent me a card last week, just to let me know she was all right. Here we are —Tidewell House, Tidemore, York. In the country, she said. I was to let her know how Horace was, but perhaps you'd be kind enough to do that if he's going with you?'

She glanced at the professor; he seemed, in the last few minutes, to have got younger, or perhaps it was because she hadn't got her glasses on.

'Certainly I'll tell her, Mrs Coffin; I shall be going back to London with him this evening.'

'All that way!' marvelled Mrs Coffin, who didn't believe in travel. 'You'll give her my love, won't you, sir?' She produced Horace's basket and he stowed him inside. 'Such a dear girl, and never a grumble, though she looked that sad.'

'Then I must find her and do my best to cheer her up,' declared the professor blandly, and bade Mrs Coffin goodbye.

He drove himself back to his house, ate the meal Trudy had got for him, fed Horace and telephoned his registrar, to be told that a severe head injury sustained by a little girl in a street accident had just been admitted and would need surgery. 'Otherwise everything's fine,' observed his right hand.

The professor suppressed impatience. 'I'm on my way in ten minutes or so. I'll come in as soon as I get back.' They discussed the case for a few minutes and he hung up. 'I'll have to get back,' he told Trudy, 'but first I must tell you that I know where Suzannah is; as soon as I'm able, I'll go to York and fetch her.'

'You don't know why she went?'

He shook his head. 'No. Though I think I can guess.' He gave her a hug. 'I'll be in touch, Trudy.'

It was almost eleven o'clock by the time he got home. He handed Horace over to Cobb, told him that he would be at the hospital if he was wanted, assured him that Suzannah was safe, and took himself off to the intensive care unit. He spent the greater part of the night operating on the child and, satisfied with his work, went home at last to sleep like a log.

He was back at the hospital in the morning, to find the child greatly improved and nothing urgent waiting for him. 'I'm going up to York,' he told his registrar. 'I've a couple of patients to see at my rooms, and I'll leave my address with Mrs Long—you can always get me in the car. I want to leave very early in the morning, and if all goes well I shall be back here in the evening of the next day.'

Thrusting all thought of his Suzannah from his mind, he worked without pause all day, catching up on letters, seeing his patients and doing a quick round at the hospital, but once home again he allowed himself to think of her. 'We really can't go on like this, can we?' he asked the faithful Henry, and Henry, who hadn't been allowed to travel down to Great Chisbourne, thumped his tail in agreement. The professor bent to stroke him. 'You shall come with me to York,' he promised. 'I dare say I shall need all the moral support I can muster.'

The pair of them left very early the next morning. It

was a cold, bleak day, but the roads were dry and the Bentley made light of the miles. The professor stopped at a service station after a couple of hours, and then drove on into a day which was now almost as dark as the night, with thick clouds racing across the steel-grey sky and a fine rain beginning to fall. But presently the rain ceased, and by this time he had almost reached York and the sky was clearing.

'A good omen, Henry,' observed the professor to the little dog curled up on the seat beside him.

He had no need to go into the centre of York but skirted its edges, and after a few miles turned off the main road and took a narrow lane which led him to Tidemore. Tidewell House, he was informed when he stopped to ask, was less than a mile along the road, and he found it easily enough; a farmhouse at one time, it was now a comfortable dwelling set in a good-sized garden with paddocks on either side. He drove up the short drive and got out, rang the old-fashioned bell beside the solid front door and waited, the picture of calm patience, for it to be opened.

He said to the rather severe elderly woman who opened it, 'Is Mrs Meredith at home? I should like to speak to her.'

'She's in. What name shall I give, sir?'

'Bowers-Bentinck.'

She ushered him inside and opened a door in the hall. The room he entered was small and only partly furnished, with packing cases lining a wall. He contemplated them without much interest, seething with an inward impatience now, and it was with relief that he heard the door open and turned to see Mrs Meredith.

They shook hands while he made the usual civil

excuses for disturbing her. 'I believe you have Miss Lightfoot working for you; I am anxious to see her.'

Mrs Meredith, airy-fairy though she was, had sharp eyes; not a man to show his feelings, she decided, but boiling over inside. 'Yes, she's here—how fortunate you came today, for my permanent nanny is returning tomorrow and Suzannah is going back. She's out with the children, but they'll be back any minute. Have you come a long way?'

'London.' He hesitated. 'I hope to take her back with me, if that would be possible?'

'I don't see why not.' She smiled at him, scenting romance in the air. 'I'll get a coat and go and meet them, and take over the children and leave you free to talk.' She was half-way to the door. 'She's been marvellous—I don't know what I'd have done without her, and the children love her. I won't be a moment.'

They went through the house, out of the back door and through the door in the garden wall. There was a paddock beyond and fields. The professor came to a halt and heaved a great sigh; his Suzannah was in the field, tossing a ball to the two children with her; they were shouting and screaming and racing around her, and Mrs Meredith and the professor were quite close before she looked up and saw them.

She stood, the ball fallen from her hand, staring at him, her mouth open, the colour creeping into her face and then ebbing away, leaving it pale. She said in a squeaky voice, 'How did you get here?'

'In the car. Hello, Suzannah.' He had come to a halt before her and took her hands in his, and neither he or Suzannah noticed Mrs Meredith dragging the children back to the house.

'How did you find me?' she whispered.

'It wasn't too difficult, my darling—your hair—people notice it. What did Phoebe say to make you run away?'

She gave her hands a little tug, but he tightened his gentle hold, and when she looked up into his face she could see that she would have to answer him. 'Well,' she began, 'she said that you and she were going to be married and that you were sorry for me and felt that you had to help me and that I was an embarrassment to you . . .'

She sniffed and her eyes filled with tears.

'Oh, dear, oh, dear,' said the professor at his most soothing. 'And, of course, you believed her.'

'Well, I didn't want to, only you didn't seem to like me . . .'

'My dearest love, I not only like you, I love you. I fell in love with you the very first time we met, but I must confess that I didn't realise it for some time, although I was plagued by an urge to look after you from the moment Phoebe told me that she had sacked you. But you refused my help in no uncertain manner, didn't you? It was then that you took possession of my heart and mind.'

'You never said anything,' she said sharply. She gave another tug and he laughed softly.

'Don't get cross, my darling; several times I thought I would take a chance, and always you backed away and started talking about the weather. But now no more of that. Will you marry me, Suzannah? And I want the answer now, so don't start arguing!'

'I never . . .' She began and saw the look in his eyes. 'Oh, Guy, of course I'll marry you, and I'm sorry I ran away, only I love you and I thought that you didn't love me . . .'

The professor let her hands go at last and wrapped his great arms around her. 'And that, my darling, is something I must disprove to you.'

He kissed her slowly and then quite fiercely, so that she had no breath to speak, only just enough to kiss him back.

The sun had gone in and a fine drizzle was drifting down. Suzannah couldn't have cared less; she was in heaven, and as for the professor, that most observant of men, he hadn't even noticed; he had his heart's desire.

HARLEQUIN
Romance®

Coming Next Month

#3055 INTENSE INVOLVEMENT Jenny Arden
Elise looks forward to a break from hospital routine on a new assignment in the Loire valley as physiotherapist to Luc de Rozanieux. Then she meets Luc and finds he's arrogant, short-tempered and extremely demanding. Extremely disturbing, too....

#3056 NOW AND FOREVER Elizabeth Barnes
When Angus O'Neil lands his hot-air balloon in Mari Scott's meadow, he breaks into her solitary life. Despite falling in love, they make no commitments. And when Angus, overcoming his fears, proposes marriage—Mari's problems keep her from saying yes!

#3057 HOME SAFE Kate Denton
The last thing Lee expects to find at her grandmother's house is a stranger living there. And a maddeningly attractive one, at that. But Allen Hilliard has a knack for turning Lee's expectations—and her life—upside down.

#3058 IMPULSIVE BUTTERFLY Kay Gregory
Jet Kellaway is tired of her years flitting from job to job—and the meager existence it provides. Things certainly change when she goes to see Seth Hagan of Hagan's Employment Agency and he decides to take her in hand!

#3059 COUNTRY BRIDE Debbie Macomber
Why wouldn't Luke Rivers believe Kate when she told him she hadn't *meant* to propose to him? She was still in love with another man! But Luke didn't believe that either....
(Sequel to *A Little Bit Country*, Harlequin Romance #3038)

#3060 MAN OF THE HOUSE Miriam MacGregor
Kay is quite happy with her very full, busy life until Rolf Warburton arrives to disrupt everything and puts her future in question. And she can't understand how she can be so attracted to him—a man she doesn't trust....

Available in June wherever paperback books are sold, or through Harlequin Reader Service:

In the U.S.
901 Fuhrmann Blvd.
P.O. Box 1397
Buffalo, N.Y. 14240-1397

In Canada
P.O. Box 603
Fort Erie, Ontario
L2A 5X3

Have You Ever Wondered If You Could Write A Harlequin Novel?

Here's great news—Harlequin is offering a series of cassette tapes to help you do just that. Written by Harlequin editors, these tapes give practical advice on how to make your characters—and your story—come alive. There's a tape for each contemporary romance series Harlequin publishes.

Mail order only

All sales final

TO: **Harlequin Reader Service**
Audiocassette Tape Offer
P.O. Box 1396
Buffalo, NY   14269-1396

I enclose a check/money order payable to HARLEQUIN READER SERVICE® for $9.70 ($8.95 plus 75¢ postage and handling) for EACH tape ordered for the total sum of $_____.*
Please send:

☐ Romance and Presents   ☐ Intrigue
☐ American Romance   ☐ Temptation
☐ Superromance   ☐ All five tapes ($38.80 total)

Signature_____
                                        (please print clearly)
Name:_____
Address:_____
State:_____ Zip:_____

*Iowa and New York residents add appropriate sales tax.

AUDIO-H